# Death at a Diner

**A Myrtle Clover Cozy Mystery, Volume 20**

Elizabeth Spann Craig

Published by Elizabeth Spann Craig, 2022.

This is a work of fiction. Similarities to real people, places, or events are entirely coincidental.

DEATH AT A DINER

**First edition. July 15, 2022.**

Copyright © 2022 Elizabeth Spann Craig.

Written by Elizabeth Spann Craig.

In memory of Amma and Daddy

# Chapter One

Myrtle said with great satisfaction, "This is the most fun I've had in forever."

Miles raised his eyebrows. "Sitting on your front porch while counting cars?"

"Just the mere act of being out here makes me feel exhilarated, Miles. I feel *free*. And I'm winning the car game. I have more red cars than you have silver cars."

Miles didn't seem very distraught over losing the game. "It's rather surprising there aren't more silver cars in Bradley. I'm certain I've read an article stating it is the most popular color for consumers. It doesn't show dirt as much, apparently."

"But red cars are more fun, aren't they? People like to have fun, even if it's just sitting in a red car."

Miles quirked an eyebrow. "Or sitting on a front porch?"

"It's the context. We're on the porch and we know Erma isn't going to pop over and fill us in on her latest, most disgusting medical condition. She's out of town! And it's absolutely marvelous."

Miles frowned. "She'll be back at some point, though. It's not as if she moved away."

"Don't be a killjoy, Miles. It's unbecoming. Think how much fun we've had in the last few days—counting cars, waving at people from the porch. And it's all been very annoying to Red how I've been able to note all his comings and goings. I've even been able to comment on what groceries he's brought into the house and suggested he cut back on his red meat consumption."

"I'm sure that pleased him to no end," said Miles.

"He knows he needs to watch his blood pressure. I absolutely love my front porch. I think I like it even more than my dock on the lake."

"Hellooooo there!" said a sudden, odious voice floating over from next door. "Myrtle? Miles? Is that you?"

Myrtle's eyes widened in horror. "It's her."

Miles looked equally alarmed. "Erma's back."

"Hurry! Let's run."

It said something about how abominable Erma was that they both scrambled to get inside Myrtle's house. Miles was holding the door open for Myrtle when, in her haste, her foot slipped and she fell, with a plunk, onto her knee.

"Myrtle?" gasped Miles.

"I'm fine, I'm fine. Help me get inside."

But it was too late as Erma was already upon them. She gaped at the two of them and then peered at Myrtle, who appeared to be having a medical issue of her own for once.

"I'll get Red," said Erma with determination.

"Nooooooo!" commanded Myrtle.

But it was too late. Erma had bounded across the street to alert Myrtle's son and the town of Bradley's police chief that his mother had fallen down.

"Get me up," gritted Myrtle between her teeth. "This problem is only cosmetic."

Miles carefully slid his arm around her and gently lifted her up from the cement floor of the porch and into her house.

Once he had her settled on the sofa, he more closely inspected her knee. "You've skinned it."

Myrtle sighed. "As if I were six and learning to ride a bike. You'll find antiseptic and bandages in my medicine cabinet, Miles. Would you mind bringing them to me?"

Just then, Red burst in through her front door with Erma close behind him, staring with wide eyes at the scene in front of her.

Myrtle was most unhappy at Erma for both returning from town and alerting Red to Myrtle's tumble. She said, "Erma, don't you have some unpacking to do?"

Erma snapped her fingers. "My cooler. Gotta put that stuff in the fridge."

"Thanks for your help," said Red as Erma gave them a wave and headed out.

Myrtle grimaced at the notion that Erma could be of any help to anyone at any time.

Red came over to take a look at Myrtle's knee, which was doing an excellent job of making it look as though Myrtle had been seriously injured.

"I skinned it," she said with a shrug. "It's as simple as that."

"Yes, but the *underlying* issue is that you lost your balance and fell," said Red grimly.

"I'll get the antiseptic," said Miles, suddenly eager to get away.

Myrtle shot Red a look. "I only fell because of the circumstances. I would never have fallen if I hadn't been trying to escape the clutches of the pernicious Erma. Desperation made this happen."

"Falls are devastating for people your age," said Red. "I just want you to be safe." He paused. "I've been waiting for the right time to tell you something. There's something I want to give you."

Miles returned with the antiseptic, cotton balls, and bandages.

"Excellent timing, Miles. I believe Red is about to propose," said Myrtle dryly.

Red shot her a look. But then he proceeded to bring out a box.

Myrtle raised her eyebrows and Red opened it to reveal a long silver necklace with an obelisk of some sort at the end.

Red cleared his throat. "It came with a chain that wasn't very pretty so I found one that looked better. That looked more like jewelry."

Myrtle took the necklace from him and studied it carefully as Miles dabbed at her knee with antiseptic and put ointment on it.

"I do believe this is a medic alert necklace," said Myrtle thoughtfully.

Red nodded. "It is. The idea is that if you fall or feel sick, you just press the button and it dials the service. Elaine and I are picking up the tab for the monitoring."

Myrtle considered the necklace some more and then carefully put it around her neck. "I thought, considering the short distance between our houses, that I could perhaps simply yell from the floor and you could hear me."

Red shook his head. "My hearing isn't what it used to be, Mama."

"Too many loud concerts when you were younger," said Myrtle promptly.

"Maybe. Besides, Jack is often making such a racket that it would be impossible to hear over him."

As usual, Myrtle didn't want to hear a word against her beloved grandson. "Happy playing sometimes means loud playing."

"Sometimes it's not happy playing at all. Sometimes it's good old-fashioned temper tantrums." He shrugged. "Anyway, this will make me feel a lot better that you can get the help you need, if you need it."

"There are phones," said Myrtle in the tone of someone informing someone else of something they didn't know.

"Sometimes people fall and their phones are out of reach," said Red. "That happened to Miz Nelson the other day."

Myrtle pursed her lips but didn't say anything. Miles carefully put a bandage over her knee.

"How does it feel?" asked Miles, regarding his work uncertainly.

Myrtle said, "Like a skinned knee. But at least it's all cleaned up. Thank you, Miles."

Red said, "Yes, thanks, Miles. And no more running, Mama. It is just lucky that you're built so sturdily."

She shrugged. "I don't *often* run. Only when the circumstances warrant it."

Red said, "Okay. Well, I'm out of here. Take it easy for a change, Mama."

As soon as the door closed behind him, Miles said, "It's very interesting that you haven't taken the necklace off and thrown it across the room yet. That fall must have shaken you up more than I thought. Are you sure you're not concussed?"

Myrtle looked down at the silver necklace. "I'm planning on keeping it on. It's the only piece of jewelry Red has ever given me. Aside from one made from painted macaroni in kindergarten, that is. And I might still have that one in my jewelry box."

"It's an attractive necklace, I must say. Probably much better than the macaroni one."

Myrtle fingered it. "It is. And it will go with all of my outfits. It's actually sort of thoughtful of him. When he blustered over here, I thought he was going to make another horrid pitch for my banishment to Greener Pastures Retirement Home."

"Do you think he's given up entirely on that idea?"

Myrtle snorted. "No way. But I suppose he doesn't think he'll have any luck in persuading me any time soon."

"I rather thought he was going to move you there last month."

Myrtle said, "Oh, you mean after the insurrection?"

Miles smiled. "The very one. And you should take more credit, considering you instigated the insurrection."

"I simply pointed out that Greener Pastures needed to devote more of their revenue stream to food. When I had dinner with Dinah Bridgeton last month, the inmates were given a single hotdog with no bun and a scrap of garlic bread. Appalling!"

Miles said, "Perhaps the fact that you refer to them as 'inmates' instead of 'residents' also created a stir."

"It makes them think, doesn't it? Thinking is always a good thing. Anyway, Dinah emailed me and said that the food has gotten better over the last week. No more salty mac and cheese and too-crunchy fish sticks. And that's what I told Red—I helped promote *progress* at Greener Pastures. The residents should throw a special ceremony for me."

Then her face fell and she sighed. "The insurrection was the highlight of my month and this is the lowlight. Erma has returned home. I was so *happy* sitting out on my front porch."

Miles said helpfully, "Sitting on the dock is nice too, though. And those bushes you planted last year really help shield you from Erma's prying eyes."

"Precisely. I couldn't stand the thought of Erma popping by all the time. She's one of those people who just doesn't take a hint." Myrtle frowned suddenly and stood, peering out her front window. "What's all this?" she asked in an irritated voice.

Miles joined her. Red was talking to Erma in a rather animated way. Erma was nodding delightedly. Red gestured toward Myrtle's house and Erma nodded again before saluting. Red patted Erma on the arm and headed back across the street to his house.

"What was all that about?" asked Miles.

Myrtle's eyes narrowed. "That little pantomime indicates that Red has recruited Erma to look after me. To *spy* on me."

"Surely not," Miles demurred. "He knows how distasteful you find Erma."

"*Everyone* finds Erma distasteful. Red is just looking to get on my nerves by having Erma hang out as close as possible. That's very annoying." Myrtle picked up her phone.

Miles said, "I have the feeling you're summoning Dusty to put out a large gnome display."

"Most certainly," said Myrtle crisply.

She punched in the numbers and heard Dusty howl on the other end, "Too dry to mow, Miz Myrtle!"

"There's no mowing required, Dusty, so you can just settle yourself down."

"Them gnomes, then?"

Myrtle said, "Yes. I'd like the gnomes set out in the front yard all in rows like a miniature army."

"What's he done now?" Dusty asked curiously.

"Red is trying to run my life, as per usual. When can you get over here to help me out?"

Dusty said, "Have to check my calendar."

"I find it very hard to believe that you maintain a calendar. Besides, I can tell that you're free right now—I hear a game show playing in the background. You can bring your wife with you, too. I'm going to be hosting book club and I need Puddin over to clean. My dust bunnies are rapidly procreating."

Dusty muttered something on the other end and Myrtle said, "See you two shortly, then." She hung up the phone.

Miles said thoughtfully, "I'd almost forgotten about the up-coming book club meeting."

"You've read the book though, surely. You're practically the only one in the club who I can count on to actually read the selection."

Miles nodded. "Of course I have. I'd read *Little Women* when I was a kid, of course, but I read it again a few weeks ago. I'd forgotten how much humor the book had and how strong the characters were. It was fun to reread it."

"I'm glad. Of course, I was forced to pick something at the book club's reading level. I've given up on my lofty goals of reading Shakespearean plays or Dostoevsky. Actually, I wondered if *Little Women* might be too difficult for this group. I'd previously contemplated assigning *Go, Spot, Go* to the group."

Miles grinned. "I think I remember how that story goes. *See spot run. Go, Spot, go. Look, look, look.*"

"That's the plot in a nutshell," said Myrtle with a sniff.

Miles said, "Did I read in one of Tippy's emails that there was a new member of book club? Or two?"

"That's right. That horrid Palmer woman has joined."

Miles raised his eyebrows. "What makes her so horrid?"

"She's just ghastly. You'll understand when you see her. She's rapidly joining every organization in town so I have to encounter her at garden club, too. She's even infiltrated church," said Myrtle gloomily.

"You're not at church very frequently," pointed out Miles in a helpful manner.

"I religiously attend online."

"No pun intended," said Miles.

"Anyway, she's going to be part of our book club now and that means it will be her turn to pick a book. Who knows what atrocious title she'll force us all to read? I may have to plan on being ill next month so I don't have to deal with it. Plus, she's bringing a friend with her. Whitney. No, Whit*ley*. I'm sure to get her name wrong." Myrtle's voice indicated that she thought Whitley had deliberately chosen her name just to annoy everyone.

"At least you're hosting this month so you'll have more control over the function. And remember," added Miles quickly,

"Book club has the new rule that the host is exempted from preparing food for the meeting."

"Yes, yes. I remember. It seems a silly sort of rule, though. I'm sure the etiquette experts would think book club is woefully falling down on the job. The whole point of being a host is to provide food and beverages to those visiting in our homes. Anyway, I suppose that's fine. I have enough to deal with getting Dusty and Puddin over here."

Miles said with a frown. "Book club is tomorrow, is it not?"

"It certainly is. It sneaked up on me, too. I should have started my campaign to get Puddin over here much earlier."

"I never understand why you continue putting up with Puddin. You could easily switch over to her cousin, Bitsy. She always seems like she does a good job. Besides, Bitsy is an avid gossip. She could provide all sorts of entertaining tidbits for you."

Myrtle said, "The problem is that I simply can't *afford* Bitsy. You've heard me say how restricting a retired teacher's budget is. Puddin is the best I can do. At any rate, she's better than me trying to chase my own dust bunnies." She gave a big sigh. "I'm all keyed up now, thinking about Erma and Red. There's only one thing to do."

Miles looked at her questioningly.

"Watch our soap opera," said Myrtle simply.

And so they did. That particular episode of *Tomorrow's Promise* was full of drama. An older character, Ralph, who'd been dealing with dementia for several months was suddenly fine and having a spirited affair with someone named Deanna.

"This show is such a hot mess," said Miles. "Their plots are a disaster. How could anyone not correct all the storyline inconsistencies? They must be changing their writers every few weeks."

"Shh!" said Myrtle. "Ralph is going to ask Deanna to marry him."

"He's seventy-five! She's thirty. And he has dementia."

Myrtle said, "But you're riveted, aren't you? That's the only thing that matters."

And so they spent the rest of the hour watching all sorts of shenanigans on *Tomorrow's Promise*. Following that, Myrtle suggested they play hearts.

Miles frowned. "I don't think two people can play hearts. I think you need three or four."

"I'll look it up online. I bet we can make some sort of modification to make it work."

Sure enough, if they removed all the 3s, 5s, 7s, 9s, Jacks, and Kings, then the game would work for two players.

Miles said in a grumbling voice, "I feel like I don't have any cards at all."

"Don't be silly. You have plenty of cards. Thirteen, as a matter of fact."

Miles became a lot jollier after that when he realized his thirteen cards made for a very good hand indeed. He had lots of spades and no queen of spades. He ended up winning the hand.

"I haven't played hearts for forever," he said. "We should do this more often."

Myrtle said, "We really should be doing this with Wanda. You know how much she loves playing cards."

Which was precisely when the phone rang. Myrtle picked up and heard Wanda's voice grating in her ear. "Yer in danger."

# Chapter Two

"Me? I think your gift is a wee bit off today. I *was* in danger—Erma Sherman unexpectedly came back into town and I fell trying to flee. But now I'm just fine. We were just talking about you—Miles and I are playing cards and thinking of you."

Wanda's voice was persistent. "Not the fall. Somethin' else. Gotta be careful."

Myrtle sighed. "This is the problem with the Sight, Wanda. It's a very vague thing. Is the danger from a person? A bad bit of seafood? A drunk driver? When it's this indefinite, I feel as if I've got to be alert from peril from all directions. It's most stressful."

Wanda said slowly, "It ain't how the Sight works."

"Yes, I know. It's still all very annoying, though." Myrtle paused. "You wouldn't happen to want to come down and play cards would you? Miles would be delighted to pick you up."

Miles's face, however, was something less than delighted.

Wanda said, "Can't today. Gotta bunch of customers comin' up."

"Oh, to get their palms read? Well, that certainly sounds lucrative. What kind of group is it?"

"Some sorta hen party," said Wanda.

"Well, hopefully you don't see anything too dire. They're probably all expecting to hear they're about to discover their one true love. Instead, you'll end up telling them they need to go to the doctor because they're about to get shingles. At any rate, it's good you're getting some business. Which reminds me—I'll need to get the horoscopes from you soon."

"Phone's gonna die," said Wanda in a very straightforward manner.

"Now? Well, hang up with me and charge it."

"No—gonna die soon and I'll need a new one."

Myrtle said, "Well then, I'll just drive up and see you then. Take care, Wanda." She hung up. "Wanda seems to need a new cell phone."

Miles gave her a gloomy look. "I suppose I'll be funding that new phone."

"Not at all. Remember, that's the phone Sloan provided to her so they could get her horoscopes in a timely fashion. He'll simply need to give her a replacement. I'll follow up with him about it."

The two continued playing Hearts and then ended up making themselves grilled cheese sandwiches for dinner before watching an intriguing, although rather confusing, documentary on black holes.

"What is mass again?" asked Myrtle with a frown.

Miles answered, "It's a matter of physics. Basically, it's the resistance—"

"You can stop right there. I can tell it's one of those definitions that ends up being harder to understand than the word itself."

Miles said, "That's nothing compared to the distortion of the space-time fabric."

"There's only one thing that will fix my confusion, Miles. A game show."

Which was when they ended up watching *Wheel of Fortune*.

The afternoon and evening had been so unexpectedly absorbing that it wasn't until quite late that Myrtle realized Dusty and Puddin hadn't made an appearance.

"Those two!" she bellowed. "I'll give them a piece of my mind."

But when she called them on the phone, they didn't answer.

"Maybe something came up," said Miles with a shrug.

"Of course it didn't! This is par for the course for those two. They didn't feel like coming. They'll probably show up tomorrow morning acting as if they didn't understand my instructions. I have book club tomorrow and Puddin will likely still be slouching around, doing my housekeeping in slow motion."

Miles said, "I should get back home and get some rest. It's going to be a busy day tomorrow." He was especially ready to escape since it appeared Myrtle would be stewing over the disappearance of Dusty and Puddin for some time.

And indeed she did. She was up all night glaring at the ceiling and completely awake. Ordinarily she'd walk down to Miles's house to wake him up and sit around doing puzzles. But she refrained from doing it this time. He had seemed tired, after all. She congratulated herself for her restraint and thoughtfulness.

Instead, she called Dusty and Puddin. It was three a.m. and she knew the two of them would certainly not still be out painting the town. All of Bradley's local attractions closed for the night at midnight.

Puddin answered the phone in a panic. "What's goin' on?"

"What's going on is that I'm fretting over my messy house and can't sleep, Puddin. I thought I'd share my insomnia with you."

"It's the middle of the night!"

Myrtle said, "Welcome to my world. I only wish I *could* sleep, but I'm so worried about book club coming over to my untidy home that I can't do it."

Puddin grumbled something that Myrtle couldn't quite make out. Then she said, more clearly, "Guess I'll come by in the morning."

"It's morning now," Myrtle pointed out helpfully. "And you're awake."

"I ain't cleanin' nothin' at this time of the mornin'."

Myrtle said, "Aha! That's a double negative, Puddin. So you *will* clean something at this hour."

Puddin seemed to be at the end of her rope now. "Talk English, Miz Myrtle."

"That's what I'm doing. Oh, never mind. Come by as soon as you can this morning, Puddin. I don't have time for any of this nonsense. And make sure Dusty is in the car with you. I need those gnomes put out asap."

Puddin hung up abruptly, still muttering to herself.

Myrtle, having resolved her housework, managed to fall into a lovely, albeit short, sleep.

It was lucky for Dusty and Puddin that they did come by the house at a fairly early hour. Neither of them looked as if they were accustomed to being up and about at that time. Dusty had the biggest Styrofoam cup of coffee that Myrtle had ever seen—and a straw protruding from it. Myrtle had never seen anyone gulp coffee through a straw before but Dusty appeared to be mastering the activity.

"Hi there, Dusty!" she called out cheerfully from her front porch.

Dusty muttered something under his breath and lifted his hand in a short wave.

"It's a pity they can't figure out a way to infuse people with a coffee IV, isn't it?" asked Myrtle.

Dusty said in a pointed way, "If you get good sleep, you don't need as much coffee."

Myrtle raised an eyebrow. "I suppose. But if you'd come yesterday, as I indicated you should, then you wouldn't have had to be here this morning."

Puddin' slouched toward Myrtle's house, her pale face showing her deep unhappiness at the prospect of chasing Myrtle's dust bunnies around.

"Where are your cleaning supplies?" asked Myrtle, scowling ferociously at her cleaning woman.

"Yonder," said Puddin, nodding indifferently toward Dusty's truck.

"Then I suggest you go find them. Mine are in low supply after you used them last time and my budget for the week doesn't include replacing them."

Puddin made a scoffing noise, whether at the accusation she'd used the supplies up or at the fact that Myrtle used a working budget, it wasn't clear.

"What're we doin' with them gnomes now?" asked Dusty, a distasteful look on his face.

"Like I said before—you're setting them out in lines like an army. Not just randomly like you usually do. I want them set out with military precision, facing Red's house."

Dusty nodded and wordlessly stomped off to start the chore.

Myrtle went back into the house to see how Puddin was coming along. It turned out she was moving very sluggishly and was hovering around Myrtle's coffee pot. She shot Myrtle a look when she came in.

Myrtle sighed. "Grab some coffee if it'll help you stay on track, Puddin. I can't invite these women over to my house with it being in such a state. Can you imagine Tippy Chambers here right now?"

Puddin squinted into the living room as if trying to picture the elegant woman in those surroundings. She shrugged and emptied the dregs of the coffee into Myrtle's largest coffee cup.

"I'm surprised you didn't make Dusty get you a coffee when he was there at the gas station getting his."

Puddin shrugged again. "Gas station coffee is gross. It ain't never fresh."

"There you go with the double negatives again," said Myrtle. "I'm starting to feel a pull toward returning to the classroom and teaching English again."

Puddin said, "Kinda old for that, Miz Myrtle. Kids is different now."

"I would argue with you, but I don't have the time. I need you to leap into action now."

Puddin, far from leaping, ambled into the living room to assess what needed to be done. Then she headed in the direction of Myrtle's back hall where the vacuum cleaner lived in a small closet.

"If you dust first, then you can vacuum up all the dust you pushed off the tables," said Myrtle in a knowledgeable manner.

There were growling noises coming from Puddin's direction, but she did stomp back out and start dusting with a sad-looking cloth from her own collection of supplies.

Having motivated her staff, Myrtle retreated to her bedroom for a few minutes to make a phone call. If she made it from the living room, she'd be subjecting herself to Puddin gossiping about her call to everyone.

Her editor, Sloan Jones, picked up the phone. "*Bradley Bugle*," he said.

"Sloan? It's Myrtle Clover."

Myrtle could hear his squeaking desk chair as Sloan likely straightened up to prepare for a conversation with his old English teacher.

"Miss Myrtle! What a pleasure. Are you calling me with your latest helpful hints column?"

Myrtle made a face. "No, I'm not," she said with displeasure.

"Oh, that's too bad. I've been meaning to let you know how much fan mail we got after your last column. It was a real hit."

Myrtle said sourly, "I think it says something about our readership that they are so excited about cleaning tips."

"Miss Myrtle, they were *so* excited. But why wouldn't they be? They thought it was great that they could clean with a product they already had in their homes—cooking spray! Who'd have thought that you can use it to clean faucets, a bathtub, *and* stop doors from squeaking? They thought that was revolution-ary."

Myrtle said darkly, "Of *course* they would love that. The problem is, Sloan, that I'm wanting to aim much higher than cleaning tips. I want to cover a *big* story."

When Sloan spoke again, he sounded rather anxious. "There's nothing going on right now, Miss Myrtle. You know how Bradley is. Sometimes stuff is happening and sometimes it's dead. Right now, it's dead."

"That means something is right on the verge of happening. It's never dead here for very long. Believe me—I've been an ob-server of the news cycles here for many decades."

Considering Myrtle was an octogenarian and a lifelong res-ident of Bradley, North Carolina, no one was going to dispute that. Sloan said hastily, "I'm sure you're right. When there is a big story, you'll get it."

"The only problem is that I'm not inclined to wait. Waiting is the bane of my existence. How about, in the meantime, I cover the upcoming town hall meeting?"

Sloan now sounded even more agitated. "Unfortunately, that story is already spoken for. Angel Aames is writing it."

"Angel Aames writes on a fourth grade reading level," said Myrtle with a sniff. "And, remember, I'm a good friend of Tippy Chambers. In fact, I'm seeing Tippy later today for book club. Perhaps I could get some interesting quotes from her for the piece." Tippy had been elected to town hall and was, in Myrtle's view, an excellent community servant.

Sloan said, "I think it would be better if we got you to cover something else."

Myrtle mulled this over for a second. "Maybe I could go on special assignment. I could be an undercover operative."

Sloan was apparently surprised into silence by this idea.

Myrtle continued, "I could infiltrate Greener Pastures retirement home. That way, I'd be undercover and could get the scoop as to what really goes on there."

Sloan said unhappily, "Miss Myrtle, Red has filled me in on your activities over there. I think it would be tough for you to be undercover. You appear to be a known entity at the home."

Myrtle sighed. "Then we're going to have to think on it, Sloan. Let's just put it this way: until I get an important assignment, I'm going to hold the helpful hints column hostage. Now I've got to run. I need to make sure my yardman and housekeeper are doing what they're supposed to. And, by the way, you need to replace Wanda's phone."

She rang off and hobbled as quickly as possible back into the living room. Puddin was staring idly out the window, apparently daydreaming.

"Puddin!" said Myrtle sternly. "Snap out of it. This house isn't going to clean itself."

Puddin, after jumping in surprise, said sullenly, "Ain't we runnin' out of time? When is that book club of yours?"

"We are *not* running out of time. You're stalling. Book club starts in an hour. Considering the size of my house, that's plenty of time to vacuum, clean the bathroom, and touch up the kitchen. Good grief, Puddin, it's not rocket science. I'd do it myself if I weren't extremely old."

Puddin had been to book club in the past and had enjoyed the free food and beverages. She'd proved something of a hit with the ladies during the discussion section when she'd parroted some insights Myrtle had given her. Myrtle had absolutely no plans on reintroducing Puddin to the club.

Puddin slung her dust rag around a tabletop, narrowly missing one of Myrtle's knickknacks. "What book are y'all reading?"

"The selection this month is *Little Women*," said Myrtle, sitting down and picking up her unfinished crossword from earlier in the day.

"Huh," said Puddin. She randomly ran her cloth around another surface, leaving a trail in the dust. "That's a weird book."

"Weird? What could possibly be weird about Louisa May Alcott?"

Puddin's small eyes narrowed. "Who?"

"The author. She wasn't exactly a weird person."

Puddin said, "Sure she was. She wrote a book about short ladies. That's kind of rude."

Myrtle's head started throbbing. "It's not a book about—never mind. I believe this is yet another one of your stalling tactics. I know better than to get drawn into your foolishness. The next thing I'll know, it'll be time for the meeting to start and no cleaning will have taken place. I'm going to sit outside. Get Dusty to come find me when you're done so I can pay you both."

And with that, she retreated down to her dock overlooking the lake. The sun was glinting on the lake, birds were singing happily overhead, and Myrtle felt certain she should be able to completely relax in such an idyllic environment. That is, until she had the uncanny feeling someone was watching her.

She turned and saw Erma Sherman staring at her over the one section of the fence that didn't have a bush in front of it.

Myrtle immediately called her out on it. "I'm trying to relax, Erma. Why am I suddenly such an object of fascination?"

Erma said in an important voice, "I'm your guardian angel, Myrtle. I'm keeping an eye on you."

"Don't."

It was Myrtle's best teaching voice—the one that had frozen high school students in their tracks. It appeared to have the desired effect on Erma, too.

"Gotcha. Quiet time, right? I'll check in on you later," said Erma before disappearing.

Myrtle sighed. That Red. The gnomes Dusty was pulling out were going to be out in the front yard a long, long time. All-in-all, the day had been most irritating so far. She could only hope book club would be better.

# Chapter Three

Book club, Myrtle decided, was not off to a good start. For one thing, at least two of the women had forgotten to bring the book with them. Another hadn't "had the chance to read the book." And Palmer appeared to be irritating Myrtle's guests.

Miles walked up to Myrtle and murmured, "Is it me, or is one of the new members creating some friction?"

"She definitely is. Look at Tippy's face."

Miles and Myrtle considered the expression on the book club president's face. Tippy was flushed with what appeared to be indignation and her features reflected anger and confusion as Palmer spoke with her.

"What's going on, I wonder?" asked Miles.

Myrtle's eyes narrowed. "It appears to be a coup of some kind. I have the feeling that Palmer is wanting to take over either book club or some other organization that Tippy manages."

"Couldn't that possibly be a good thing? In terms of book club, I mean. We've never been happy with the monthly selections."

"That remains to be seen," said Myrtle with a sniff. "Palmer may decide to choose something completely insipid like everyone else does. I haven't been able to form an opinion of her yet."

"You'll have the chance to do so now," said Miles as Palmer, grinning a very white, toothy grin, strode over to see them. Her friend ,Whitley, trailed behind her.

Palmer was one of those Southern women who looked like one thing but was actually something else. A wolf in sheep's clothing, in a way. She was very blonde with piercing blue eyes, high cheekbones, and—currently—an impatient expression. Her friend, Whitley, on the other hand, was sporting a bad blonde dye which exposed quite a few dark roots. She was also very pregnant and looked rather tired.

Palmer was also one of those women who made Myrtle feel like a giantess. Myrtle was nearly six feet tall, and Palmer was very petite—maybe closer to five feet.

Palmer said, "Miss Myrtle! I wanted to come over and say hi to my hostess."

Myrtle felt the implication was there that perhaps Myrtle should have greeted Palmer first. She didn't apologize since she felt Palmer had displayed bad manners for pointing it out.

"Good to see you here Palmer, and you too, Whitley. It's delightful to have new members in the group."

Whitley laughed nervously. "I'm not much of a reader, Miss Myrtle. I hope I do all right today."

Myrtle smiled at her. "It's nice to actually hear someone take book club *seriously* for once. But don't worry, Whitley. It's not school. We're just here to enjoy books we might not have picked out for ourselves and to talk about them. You won't be put on the spot and you can be as quiet or as vocal as you'd like."

Whitley said shyly, "Speaking of school, my husband speaks very highly of you. Said you taught him for a couple of different classes."

"Who is your husband?"

"Hiram."

No last name was forthcoming or necessary because there was only one Hiram in town. "One of my most-favorite students. Tell him hi for me."

Palmer, ignoring their exchange, was already looking around Myrtle's living room with the gaze of someone planning to execute a swift and merciless takeover. "I know this club has been around for a while. I was wondering if the group would take offence if I offered some ways to improve things."

Myrtle thought that was rather brash of her, considering she was at her very first meeting. But she said, "Oh, please do make suggestions. Miles and I have tried for ages to take this book club in a different direction."

Palmer was nodding but Myrtle got the impression she wasn't listening to her. And, as a former teacher, Myrtle very much liked it when people listened to her. She narrowed her eyes.

Palmer continued. "Maybe some new leadership. I'm sure Tippy is doing a *fine* job, but her calendar has got to be overcrowded. It's crazy how much she's taken on. Town hall, church committees, book club, and garden club? I don't see how she even sleeps at night. Anyway, I was thinking we could have collaborations with a couple of the other book clubs in Bradley. Bring them together for some social time, networking, that sort of thing."

Myrtle's hopes that book club would be radically altered into a club for book aficionados were dashed. "Oh. I was just hoping we could change the type of books we were reading. Miles and I have been trying to work in classical literature with only fair to middling success. Sometimes our picks are total failures."

Palmer blinked at her as if changing the featured titles was the farthest thing from her mind. Then she suddenly said, "Oh, there's someone I need to speak with. So good to see you, Miss Myrtle." And she strode off, a diminutive dynamo on a mission.

Whitley was left behind, smiling weakly at Myrtle. Myrtle was scrambling for some sort of small talk, perhaps the old standby of the weather when Whitley said admiringly, "Isn't Palmer amazing?"

Myrtle considered this. "Well, she's certainly very motivated. I haven't known Palmer long. Could you tell me more about her?"

Whitley was clearly very impressed with Palmer in every way. "She's a real marvel. We're so lucky to have her here in Bradley."

Myrtle thought that remained to be seen.

Whitley continued in a reverent tone, "She's done the whole nine yards, you know. She was in a sorority when she was in college—one of the *best* sororities at one of the *best* universities."

Myrtle failed to look impressed by this so Whitley continued her passionate litany, "Then she was a debutante. In *Texas*. That's such a huge deal over there. Then she married well, of course. Cash, that's her husband, is just such a great guy. They live in a mansion."

"How very nice for them," said Myrtle. Myrtle had never wanted to live in a mansion. She was very happy in her own, very small home. Besides, the thought of trying to motivate Puddin to clean something that large made her shudder.

"Palmer's very *nice*, too," said Whitley. "She hosts her impoverished cousin in her backyard."

Myrtle knit her brows. "In her backyard?" She had visions of the unfortunate cousin in a pup-tent.

Whitley gave a tittering laugh. "Oh gracious, I made it sound like her cousin is roughing it. No, Cash and Palmer have a cottage on their grounds. Shay, that's the cousin, lives in the cottage. Isn't that wonderful?"

Myrtle wondered how Shay felt about being referred to as the impoverished cousin. She also wondered if Palmer herself made a point of bringing up and outlining her good deeds to others. Myrtle had always thought that bragging negated the benevolent act.

Whitley sensed Myrtle wasn't quite as impressed as she'd intended her to be. She continued, "Palmer is actually *always* helping others. She's doing all sorts of things with the homeless and the women's shelter. And she has *vision*. Ideas about how to help people and how to make groups better. She's a wonder."

Myrtle nodded politely, but watched with interest as Palmer spoke again with Tippy. Tippy's face was quite drawn. Whatever Palmer was telling her, she was decidedly unhappy about it.

"I think it's about time for us to start," said Myrtle in lieu of having to comment on Palmer being a wonder. "Would you like to take a seat, Whitley? I couldn't help but notice you're expecting—can I get you something to eat or drink before we start?"

Whitley rubbed her stomach lovingly. "Thanks, Miss Myrtle, but I ate before I came and I bring my water bottle with me wherever I go. It's in my purse." She indicated what looked like a carry-on bag that was sitting near Myrtle's front door. "I'll wait to sit down—I want to see where Palmer sits first."

Myrtle smiled and then walked to the front of the room. "Everyone?" she called in her teacher voice. "It's time for us to start talking about the book."

She assumed Tippy was going to start them off, since she was the president of the club. Tippy usually liked to say a few words and then hand the meeting back over to the host. But Tippy was decidedly not herself. She seemed distracted and the expression on her face was quite out of sorts. So Myrtle took over the intro.

"Welcome to our new members today, Palmer and Whitley."

Everyone gave a polite round of applause. Tippy tepidly joined in.

Myrtle said, "Remember our meeting next month will be at Blanche's house. I forget what the title of the book is."

That was because, in Myrtle's eyes, the title was imminently forgettable.

Blanche called out, "It's *Her Hidden Desires*."

"Right," said Myrtle, pressing her lips together in distaste.

Miles smiled in the front row.

"And now, let's move on to *Little Women*. It's a classic novel by Louisa May Alcott. Who'd like to start us off with their thoughts?" asked Myrtle.

Palmer's hand immediately shot up and Myrtle wasn't in the least surprised. It seemed very much in character for Palmer to quickly take over a meeting or to be the very first to speak out of the entire group.

"Yes, Palmer?" asked Myrtle.

Palmer said smoothly in her well-educated Southern accent, "It's an excellent portrayal of life in that particular time. Women had to be strong to deal with absent husbands away at war. There was also, of course, a focus on marriage for the girls."

Blanche interrupted Palmer, which clearly irritated her. "Yeah, but the book could just as well have been set here in the 21st century. It carries over really well."

Palmer shook her head. "It's more of a period piece. Look at Meg and her disastrous introduction to housekeeping. The focus is having women at home, married, and creating a home."

Myrtle demurred. "Nice point, Palmer, but I think the story is about far more than that. Instead of just a period piece, it demonstrates a coming-of-age theme that translates well to modern-day readers."

Palmer looked as if she wanted to debate this point so Myrtle deliberately decided to call on someone else.

Unfortunately, the person who was most eager to say something was Erma. Myrtle was sure some sort of nonsense was about to come out of her mouth.

Erma said excitedly, "Myrtle is right. It was real modern. A romance between two boys is pretty unusual for back then."

Miles closed his eyes.

Myrtle tilted her head to one side, looking at Erma through narrowed eyes. "What led you to believe there was that sort of romance going on?"

Erma snorted. "Because that boy Joe and that teacher got together at the end."

Myrtle said sternly, "Erma, the book is about little *women*."

"Yeah, that was the only part that couldn't work these days. That title. You'd have to call them 'vertically challenged' women or some such."

Myrtle didn't know where to start with this. It was appalling to her that both Erma and Puddin had similar reactions to the title of the book.

Fortunately, Georgia Simpson, she of the tattoos, big hair, and overly-mascaraed eyes, gave a booming laugh and stepped in. "Erma! You lost the whole point. The characters are little women because they're *becoming* women. And Jo is a girl. For pity's sake."

There was some tittering among the ladies. Myrtle noticed that Tippy was still distracted and didn't join in.

Erma's eyes opened wide. "Is that so? Gosh. Well, I'll have to read the book all over again. That changes everything."

"It does indeed," said Myrtle. "Does anyone else have any thoughts?" She looked meaningfully at Miles. Myrtle had a strong need for someone to say something thoughtful and academic about the story and she didn't particularly want to hear it from Palmer.

Miles cleared his throat and all the ladies beamed admiringly at him. As a widower who still drove a car, Miles was something of an alluring commodity in Bradley, North Carolina. The book club ladies fell all over themselves whenever he opened his mouth at a meeting. Ordinarily, this annoyed Myrtle to no end, but today would prove an exception.

Miles said, "This was a favorite book of mine when I was a young man and I was delighted to find that it was just as appealing to me re-reading it as an old one."

The ladies all quickly murmured their dissent that Miles was old. Myrtle hated to break it to them but seventy wasn't young.

Miles continued, "As far as the romance is concerned, I always wanted Jo to end up with Laurie. But this time, when reading the book, I realized that it wouldn't have worked out between those two. Jo looked at Laurie as a friend or, I suppose, the brother she didn't have. I don't totally buy the romance between Laurie and Amy, but that might be explained by the fact that their relationship started while they were abroad so it happened out of the reader's eyes and seemed rather sudden when it happened."

The ladies were all agog hearing Miles opine on romance. Their eyes gleamed in an enraptured manner.

Miles continued, "The professor, although he was written as much older than Jo, seemed like a good intellectual fit. And I thought their relationship seemed rather sweet."

The ladies' all said, "Ohhh," in chorus. Miles blushed a little.

Palmer, however, looked as if she completely disagreed. She was, perhaps, immune to Miles's charms, being so much younger. She quickly said, "I didn't appreciate the way the professor tried to dictate what Jo wrote. It was none of his business if she was writing pulp fiction or some kind of commercial story. I found that irritating and overbearing of him."

Miles gave Myrtle a desperate look. She smoothly said, "I disagree, Palmer. I believe the professor, Friedrich Bhaer, wanted Jo to be true to herself and write what she knew. He felt she was going to squander her talent if she got caught up in the pulp fiction mill."

Palmer's eyes narrowed. It was clear she didn't much care for dissent.

Tippy, who appeared to have recovered, stepped into her usual role of peacemaker and asked a completely innocuous question about Amy, what on earth pickled limes were, and why they were so popular in nineteenth century New England.

And so book club progressed. Palmer didn't contribute more to the discussion, which was just fine with Myrtle.

The meeting wrapped up and the ladies hurried over to tell Miles how brilliant his literary analysis was.

Palmer sauntered over to talk to Myrtle. Although she presented a tough front, Myrtle towered over her. Plus, Myrtle was in something of a cranky mood.

Palmer, however, wanted to make nice. "Thank you for hosting, Miss Myrtle. It's a very interesting club." The last was said in a most uneffusive manner.

Myrtle bristled and then was surprised by her defensive response. "The people are what makes the club special. The literary selections, aside from Miles's and mine, are remarkable only in their banality."

Palmer tilted her head to one side. "It could use a little help. I do think I could make a difference."

Myrtle lifted her eyebrows. "By all means. But be aware that others have tried and failed. You can lead a horse to water but you can't make it drink."

Palmer didn't seem to be really listening to Myrtle, which was making Myrtle even more annoyed than she already was.

"Your garden club is the same way," said Palmer.

Myrtle demurred. "I don't think garden club is remotely in the same boat as book club. It has excellent speakers and programs. The fundraisers are well-attended and the club has done some good work in the community."

Palmer shrugged. "There's always room for growth. That's what I feel passionate about, ultimately . . . making a difference. I'm passionate about so many things, of course. Especially my charity work."

Myrtle frowned. "Surely you mean *volunteering*."

Palmer looked momentarily confused. "Whatever." She spotted her friend Whitley hovering nearby and said, "We should head on out. Thanks again for hosting."

Myrtle pressed her lips together in irritation as Palmer and Whitley headed away. She could hear Palmer saying, "I always try to have respect for my elders, just like Mama taught me, but sometimes it's hard."

# Chapter Four

Miles walked up to Myrtle. "I recognize that look. Who's in trouble? Surely not Red again."

Myrtle spat out, "That Palmer. I really, really dislike her."

"You're not the only one," said Miles. "She's very opinionated, isn't she?"

"And misguided," said Myrtle. "And many other things I hesitate to even say. Plus, she seems to have some sort of Lady Bountiful complex. She volunteers in order to impress others."

Tippy said in a dry voice from behind them, "You two must be talking about our newest member to book club."

"And garden club and any other organization in this town."

Tippy said, "I'm exhausted from dealing with her. Of course I'm *glad* that someone has come in with new ideas and enthusiasm. It's especially nice that it's a young person since I think older volunteers and club leaders get over-extended. The same people get roped into volunteering and leading over and over."

Myrtle was just glad Tippy wasn't giving her any reproachful looks. Tippy had tried recruiting Myrtle into numerous other organizations, often with Red's encouragement. Red liked to keep his mother busy and out of trouble. Myrtle preferred to stay quiet and in-trouble, if at all possible.

Miles said, "It's good that you're open to new ideas, Tippy. I'm guessing the problem is the way Palmer is trying to execute them."

"Exactly," said Tippy with relief. "She's a very assertive young woman. But then, from what I understand of her background, that's a quality that's served her well. She sent me a fact sheet on herself."

Myrtle and Miles just stared at her. "What's a 'fact sheet'?" inquired Myrtle.

Tippy sighed. "It's a sort of profile outlining accomplishments."

"A curriculum vitae?" asked Miles.

Tippy nodded.

Miles asked slowly, "And she would need to present that because . . . ?"

Myrtle answered, "Because she wants to take over some leadership positions at different clubs."

Tippy nodded again.

Myrtle said, "I heard her saying some nonsense about 'Tippy taking on too much' or some such. Clearly, she's justified a coup in her mind."

Tippy sighed. "I know she's right, in a way. We do need some fresh ideas and younger volunteers, as I mentioned. I wonder if sometimes I'm involved in so many different organizations that I'm just going through the motions."

"Of *course* you're not!" said Myrtle. "You're always organized and thoughtful in your approach. You do a good job."

Miles made agreeing sounds.

Tippy looked pleased. "Thanks, you two. I needed to hear that." She glanced around and noticed most of the book club members were heading out Myrtle's front door. "I should be getting on my way. Thanks for hosting this month, Myrtle."

After everyone had cleared out, Miles said, "I'll give you a hand putting everything back to normal."

"If you don't mind pulling my kitchen chairs back into the kitchen, that would be great. I'm sure I can handle everything else."

That was precisely when the door opened again and Puddin stuck her head in. Her gaze went straight for the food table, which was still groaning with food.

"What excellent timing," purred Myrtle. "We were just saying we needed someone to help us clean up. And here you are."

Puddin shot her a sullen look. "I'm just here for my cleaning supplies that I forgot."

"I didn't see that you'd left any behind."

Puddin started walking toward the kitchen. "Of course I did." She went under Myrtle's kitchen sink and yanked out a container of bright blue cleaning solution.

Myrtle shook her head at her. "Nope. That's name-brand. You don't buy name-brand cleaners. Leave my 'Mr. Clean' alone, Puddin."

Puddin looked even more sour than she had previously.

"I suspect you're here for the free food. You invented a reason to come back and collect some leftovers."

Puddin muttered, "No reason for you to have all that food."

"I'm happy to share it with you, Puddin. But first, I need you to give us a hand. You're younger than Miles and me and it'll be easy for you to lug those kitchen chairs out of the living room."

Puddin looked conflicted. Clearly, part of her wanted to slink away and forget the entire thing. But then she looked back over at the food table.

"There's some good stuff there," said Miles.

Myrtle added, "It's very nice that the club members bring their food in disposable containers so they don't have to leave with them."

Finally won over, Puddin started dragging the chairs out of the living room while Myrtle pulled out plastic wrap and paper plates for Puddin to help herself to the spoils of the book club meeting. Miles busied himself with collecting garbage, taking it out, and replacing the trash bag.

Puddin's curiosity finally got the better of her and she grudgingly asked, "So I saw that Palmer woman was here. What's she like?"

Myrtle shrugged. "She's a little pushy. I guess she means well, though." Myrtle was in a particularly charitable mood since her meeting had been such a success.

Puddin said, "I hear people don't like her."

"Don't they?"

"No. I hear things about her."

"Yes, Puddin, that's what you've intimated. What is it precisely that you've heard?" asked Myrtle.

"That she's mean to people," said Puddin. She puffed up in the way she did when she felt important by knowing things other people didn't know.

"Mean to people," repeated Myrtle. "You're making her sound like she's in kindergarten and has tantrums when someone is hogging the blocks."

Puddin shot her a look. "Mean to that Whitley she hangs out with. The one who's expectin.'"

As if there were many Whitleys in the small town of Bradley. "Well, I'm sorry to hear that," said Myrtle.

"People have heard Palmer put her down," elaborated Puddin. "She's a bad friend. Hateful."

"Got it. Well, I'll be sure to steer clear, if possible. Although I hardly think Palmer would consider me to be good friend material. I'm somewhat out of her peer group."

Puddin lost interest in the topic and headed over to stare hungrily at the food table.

"I pulled out some containers for you to put food in for you and Dusty," said Myrtle.

Puddin snorted. "Dusty ain't getting' this. Gonna eat it before he comes back home."

"Now who's being a bad friend?" asked Myrtle.

Puddin ignored her, intent on scouring the table for the best selection.

Miles looked around him. "Everything looks put back together again, doesn't it?"

Myrtle nodded. "It doesn't take much. The ladies aren't exactly the craziest of party guests under ordinary circumstances. Most of them clean up after themselves. Erma doesn't, of course, but that's typical for Erma."

Puddin tore her attention away from the food table. "Saw her outside. Looks like she set out a chair on her front porch and was lookin' over here."

"A chair?" Myrtle sounded appalled. "What! She's going to be hanging out on her front porch now? That porch doesn't even have room for a chair?"

Puddin shrugged, losing interest in the conversation. "She made it work." She finished loading a second container with an assortment of food. "There." She looked at the containers with satisfaction.

Myrtle looked up at the clock. "You'd better head on back home with those if you're planning on consuming them in secret. Dusty isn't one to work long hours—isn't this about the time when he usually calls it a day?"

Puddin followed her gaze and looked somewhat alarmed. She scampered out of the house with her plates as if the hounds of hell were at her heels.

Miles said, "I should probably head out too, Myrtle. The house looks respectable again, everyone's gone, and that book club meeting positively wiped me out."

"Really? I thought it was an excellent meeting, all-in-all."

Miles said, "Oh, it was definitely a success. But for some reason, it exhausted me."

"Must have been all the admiring glances from the old hens at the meeting," said Myrtle. "I'd imagine it would be challenging to dodge them."

Miles gave her a crooked grin. "You know, it *is* sort of annoying."

Myrtle snickered. "You could give me a ring and you and I could say we have one of those open-ended engagements. It could go on for decades like that." She looked down at her medic alert necklace on its elegant chain. "It could go with my new necklace."

Miles brightened. "They'd leave me alone then, I bet."

"No, they wouldn't. They'd be motivated to try and steal you away from me. The older ladies in Bradley are a very competitive lot. I was just kidding, Miles."

Miles looked dejected. "Well, it was an idea, at least. Anyway, I'm heading home for a nap."

"Want to do breakfast tomorrow at the diner? I have a hankering for a breakfast sandwich with sausage, eggs, and cheese. Maybe *two* of them, actually."

Miles said, "I always wonder how you've reached your ripe old age considering what you're feeding yourself. Aren't your arteries supposed to be clogged?"

"I guess I have extra-wide arteries," said Myrtle with a shrug. "Breakfast?"

"Oh, right. Yes, let's do that."

That night, Myrtle couldn't seem to sleep a wink. She stared at the cracks on her ceiling for a while, then decided she might as well be productive and started a load of laundry. Then she picked up her book. The book, however, was far too exciting and had the opposite effect from what she intended.

She migrated over to work in her crossword puzzle book. After completing several puzzles, she looked at the clock. It was three a.m. and sleep was clearly completely elusive. Myrtle decided to visit Miles. He was quite often awake at three a.m.

Myrtle pulled on her old robe and her good slippers and headed outside and down the sidewalk toward Miles's house. Along the way she was joined by a sleek black cat who greeted her with a pleased mew.

"Pasha!" said Myrtle, equally pleased. "You brilliant girl. Were you waiting for me outside?"

Pasha smiled a feline smile up at her. She was a feral cat and Myrtle knew she didn't belong to her. Myrtle thought, perhaps, *she* belonged to Pasha. Regardless, it was always very flattering when Pasha decided to spend time with her.

Miles's house had a single light on and Myrtle said to Pasha, "That means he's awake but he wants to go back to sleep. He hasn't learned yet that it's quite impossible to fall back asleep most of the time."

She tapped on the door and listened. She thought she detected some movement in the house but no one came to the door. She tapped again, more peremptorily this time.

The door opened in a reluctant fashion and Miles stood there in his navy robe over his striped pajamas and his navy slippers.

"Pasha and I would like to visit for a while," said Myrtle smoothly. "You look wide awake, you know."

Miles opened the door wide for Myrtle and Pasha. He sighed. "I was hoping to fall back asleep."

"You don't look the least bit sleepy," said Myrtle in the manner of one who knew.

Miles made some grumbling noises but he walked into the kitchen to make coffee. "Decaf or regular?" he asked, as if there might be a big decision to be made.

"Regular, of course. There are many hours ahead of us."

Miles made the coffee and Myrtle set out some mugs, the half-and-half, and the sugar. Pasha watched them both with great interest, tail swishing.

Myrtle looked thoughtfully at Pasha. "Have any tuna, Miles?"

Miles turned a little green at the thought of tuna at three a.m. "I don't think so. I'm not such a huge fan of tuna. I might have some canned chicken. Are you needing protein? It's awfully early in the morning, isn't it?"

"No, no. I need it for *Pasha*. The poor darling looks like she's starving."

Pasha batted her eyes at Miles.

Miles muttered, "That is a well-fed cat."

"Well, if we give her some chicken, she might stop eliminating the squirrel and chipmunk population."

Miles, although he was not in the least concerned about squirrels or chipmunks, put a can of chicken on a paper plate. Pasha, far from being ravenous but very interested in the chicken, made short work of the contents of the plate.

Miles and Myrtle took their coffees into Miles's living room.

Miles rubbed his eyes. "The paper hasn't even come so I don't have any crosswords for you to work."

Myrtle waved her hand dismissively. "I've already worked several puzzles today already. Let's watch TV."

Miles blinked at her. "*Live* television?"

"Yes, Miles. We'll turn on the TV, flip through channels, and make a decision."

Miles picked up the remote with a doubtful expression on his face. "I'm not sure there's going to be much to decide from."

Sure enough, there were several infomercials, two news programs featuring very young-looking anchors who appeared to be fortified with a great deal of caffeine, and a nature show.

"The nature show is the obvious choice," said Myrtle complacently.

"We don't even know what animal it's featuring," objected Miles. "All we can see are bushes."

"I have no preference in terms of animal. Any animal will be fine today."

And so, they watched as the documentary team spent a good deal of time getting close-up video of aardwolves in east and southern Africa.

"I've never heard of an aardwolf," said Miles, sounding very awake and interested.

"Mm." Myrtle felt herself becoming very drowsy as the narrator intoned about the aardwolf's relationship to hyenas.

"They sound like very helpful little guys. Look, they eat termites."

But Miles received no response from Myrtle. She was fast asleep. Miles continued watching the program as it detailed how aardwolves survived drought conditions.

When Myrtle finally woke up, Miles was avidly watching the show that had come on after the aardwolf documentary.

"What's this one?" asked Myrtle, yawning.

"A bilby."

"Never heard of it. Looks like a possum."

Miles nodded. "It's related to them. It's a marsupial in Australia."

"Miles, what time is it?"

Miles squinted over at a clock on his far wall. He looked momentarily startled. "It's almost six o'clock."

"Well, I had a fabulous nap and I feel wonderfully refreshed. It looks as though you might not have gotten any sleep at all."

Miles looked rather deflated. "No. I found the shows too interesting."

"We could go to breakfast at this point. They'll be opening up right when we get there at the diner. If you don't think you'll go back to bed, I mean."

Miles shook his head sadly. "I'm wide awake. Maybe it'll hit me later but there's no way I'm falling asleep now."

So Myrtle headed home and Miles got ready and then the two of them headed off for the diner.

"Are we sure the diner definitely opens at six?" asked Miles. "I seem to remember we've run into this before. We've set out very early only to be disappointed to discover they opened at seven."

"Try not to be so pessimistic. I'm certain they're all over there."

"Yes, but are they over there *prepping* for breakfast or *serving* it? Those are two entirely different things," said Miles.

Sure enough, when they pulled up to the diner, the neon sign in the window said "closed." The lights were all on, however, and they could see the staff bustling around inside.

"Perhaps they open at six-thirty, not seven," said Myrtle. "Go run up to the door and take a look at the sign."

Miles sighed, got out of the car, and ambled in the direction of the front door. While he was on his mission, Myrtle amused herself by looking around the parking lot at the back of the diner. Apparently, there were already four or five people working, which was something of a surprise, considering the hour. Myrtle imagined they'd only need one server at this time of day. She wasn't sure how many fry cooks would be required, but she couldn't imagine it would be many.

One of the vehicles had its door open. Myrtle couldn't see any sign of its owner, though. Why would someone leave their driver's door open when they went into work?

Miles returned. "Myrtle, they open at seven. I think we should head over to the grocery store and pick up some eggs and bacon. I can make us a fairly decent breakfast."

Myrtle barely heard him. "See that truck over there?"

"There are several trucks," said Miles in the tone of someone who hadn't had much sleep and might be about to lose his patience.

"The fancy truck. The one with all the bells and whistles. It has its door open."

Miles shrugged. "Maybe the driver was carrying something heavy inside and was planning on returning to get another load later."

Myrtle frowned. "I think that's Palmer's truck."

Miles took a closer look at the vehicle. "I somehow can't see Palmer driving a truck."

"That's the thing. She's quite petite and might need a ladder to climb into the cab. I suspect, for her, that it might be an attention-seeking thing. It's her truck—I'm sure of it."

Miles was quiet for a moment. "What are you thinking?"

"I'm thinking we should walk right over there and see what's going on."

Miles seemed quite resistant to this idea. "Palmer doesn't seem like the type of person who might want to be interrogated at six in the morning."

"Well, that's just the problem, isn't it? What is she doing here? Why is her door open? Perhaps she's in some sort of distress." Myrtle opened her car door, gripped her cane, and headed into the darkness of the parking lot.

Miles, with a sigh, quickly followed her.

"Oh my," said Myrtle as she reached the truck a few seconds before Miles did.

Palmer Baxter was slumped across the front seat, dead.

# Chapter Five

Miles recoiled at the sight. "We should get back in the car, Myrtle. This is clearly a crime scene." He looked behind him nervously. "And the perpetrator might still be around."

"Unlikely! Who's going to kill someone and then hang around?"

Miles looked unhappy. "A psychopath."

"Well, they'll have us to contend with. Do go ahead and call Red, though, Miles. You and I will protect the crime scene until he can make it over."

Miles sighed as Myrtle used the light from her cell phone to illuminate the inside of the truck.

"Red?" he asked after dialing. "Um, how are you?" he asked, unable to prevent himself from pleasantries.

He continued, "I'm very sorry to wake you up. Yes, it does have to do with your mom, but she's fine. We're over at the diner." He paused, listening. "Yes, we now realize it's not open yet. Myrtle was sure—well, anyway, while we were in the parking lot, we discovered there was a body here."

There was something of an explosion on the other side of the line and Miles pulled the phone slightly away from his ear.

"So, anyway," Miles said after the explosion had ended, "Um, Red?"

Myrtle said crisply, "He'll have hung up so he can get his uniform on and come over here. But I have found something interesting in the meantime."

"You're not touching anything, are you? I don't think Red would be happy to find out that we not only discovered a body, but we messed up a crime scene."

Myrtle said, "Of *course* I haven't touched anything. I'm a pro."

Miles quirked an eyebrow at this statement. "I think you're the opposite of a pro."

"I'm a gifted amateur. At any rate, I've taken pictures with my flash on so that I could see what it was that Palmer was reaching for when she was hit from behind."

Miles stood next to her and she enlarged the photo. He frowned. "Some sort of notebook."

"Yes, but look what the page the notebook was open to."

Miles peered at the image more closely. "It looks like she was planning on making an offer to purchase the diner."

"And turn it into some sort of chichi café," said Myrtle. "She has bullet points there with her concept for changing the place. Removing the vinyl booths and putting café tables in. Fluffy white curtains in the windows. And changing the name from Bo's Diner to Cash's Café."

Miles said, "It sounds like quite a major upgrade."

"It sounds *atrocious*. Except for the name change, which was actually rather clever of her. Her husband is Cash, I believe. Aside from that, however, it all sounds very grim. Bo's Diner has been around for generations. I remember going there when I was a child."

Miles frowned. "You're not saying someone was unhappy about the proposal and decided to murder Palmer because of it?"

"I don't think it takes a lot of imagination to think of other reasons someone might want to kill Palmer. She was rather unlikeable. But I do believe Red will latch onto this portfolio notebook and regard it as a very important clue, indeed. But then, Red never did have very much imagination, bless his heart."

At that moment, a police car pulled into the diner parking lot at a fast clip.

"And here he is now," said Myrtle.

Red hopped out quickly, striding over to Myrtle and Miles. "Keep away from the vehicle."

Miles immediately took several large steps back. Myrtle said, "We're not even close to it. We're protecting the scene."

Red growled, "Nobody is crazy enough to come to a diner at this hour except for you, Mama. Miles, I know you were just here to drive her, which I appreciate."

He surveyed the scene and then started stringing police tape up.

"Won't you call the state police?" asked Myrtle. "It would be so nice to visit with Lieutenant Perkins this morning."

"I called them just as soon as Miles reached out to me. They should be over here soon with a forensics team."

Miles said a little anxiously, "Should I take Myrtle back home, then?"

Myrtle shot him a look.

Red looked as if he very much would like to agree with that proposal, but he shook his head regretfully. "I think the state police are going to want to have a word with you two." He paused. "Am I right in thinking this is Palmer Baxter?"

"You certainly are," said Myrtle. "I have to say I'm surprised you would know her. I wouldn't have thought you two ran in the same circles."

"We don't," said Red. "But she's out and about all the time in that truck and she has something of a lead foot. I've had to warn her about her speed a couple of times. Was she married?"

"Indeed she was," said Myrtle. "Would you like the number of her husband?"

Red frowned. "I'm surprised you'd have that sort of information at your fingertips, Mama."

"Oh, I'm full of surprises."

Red said, "If you'll just give me the address, please, if you have it. I'll dispatch my deputy to go by his house in person."

"I see. Yes, that's the kind of news one would want to deliver in person, isn't it?" Myrtle gave him the address from her contacts list.

Red nodded and pulled out his phone. "While the two of you are waiting, why don't you see if you can sit down in the diner?"

"They're not open yet," said Myrtle primly. "That's the whole reason we were hanging out in the parking lot to begin with."

Red frowned at her choice of words. "Hanging out in the parking lot makes it sound like y'all are juvenile delinquents. Here, let me walk you in there. I think they'll open their doors for me."

He made a quick call to his deputy and then escorted Myrtle and Miles to the front door of the diner. He knocked in a peremptory fashion and the doors swiftly opened for him.

"Red," said Bo, the owner, with concern. "Is everything all right?"

"No," said Red. "Unfortunately, you've had a suspicious death on your premises. I'm going to need to block off the entirety of your parking lot as a crime scene."

Bo turned pale and beads of sweat popped up on his brow. "You're saying a murder happened back there? Hey, we've all been in here the whole time doing food prep."

Red used his most patient voice, the one he never seemed to be able to summon when speaking with his mother. "I hear you, Bo. We're going to need to take statements from all of you in a bit. For now, though, I need something else from you. My mother and Miles Bradford are here and need a place to sit down. Can you let them stay here for a while?"

Bo looked a bit bemused at Myrtle and Miles's presence. "Of course. Have a seat anywhere you like."

Myrtle carefully chose a booth with an excellent view of the parking lot.

Red rolled his eyes.

Bo said hesitantly, "So are we needing to shut down for the day?"

"I wouldn't say that," said Red. "But your customers are going to need to find street parking or park out front, either way. So it's up to you."

"There's plenty of street parking," said Myrtle helpfully. "And, with all the police tape, there's sure to be lots of business. People are so nosy, you know."

Red narrowed his eyes at her.

Bo said slowly, "I guess we'll still plan on opening. I can't afford to lose a day of income."

He headed back to the kitchen and Red walked back outside to Palmer's truck.

Miles said, "This has been a very unusual morning. I wish I'd had more coffee before we left."

"Well, we'll be sure to get some once the diner officially opens for the day. We're first in line, after all. The state police can ask us their questions while we enjoy our eggs, biscuits, and sausage."

Miles looked slightly green at the thought. "I'm not at all sure I can eat anything, Myrtle. You must have a stomach made of steel."

Myrtle frowned. "Your own stomach is really quite peculiar. It's so highly sensitive that you've got to constantly baby it. You could just ask them to serve you toast. That might settle you down some. Besides, the coffee you're craving is going to be very abrasive going down. If your gut is already queasy, that's not going to help it much. You'd be better to stick with toast and ginger ale."

Miles appeared unhappy at this possibility. Which was right when their server showed up.

It was Jolene, who Myrtle had never seen without chewing gum in her mouth. Having been a teacher, Myrtle had a rather acrimonious relationship with gum.

Sure enough, Jolene was already chewing, despite the early hour. But all was forgiven when she grinned at them and said in a chipper tone, "Hi there, early birds! How about some coffee and food to shore you up while you wait?"

Miles shifted uncomfortably. "But you're not open yet."

"Sweetie, we'd be happy to serve y'all something while you wait. You did us all a favor by seeing whatever happened out there and calling the cops. I'd have been shaking in my shoes if it had been me." Jolene gave an exaggerated shudder.

"You're the best, Jolene. I'd been wanting a breakfast sandwich, but the adventure this morning is making me want to shore up some strength. I'll have a large coffee and your three-egg breakfast with sausage links, cheese grits, and hashbrowns." She glanced over at Miles. "Miles, did you figure out what you might want?"

Miles said miserably, "Toast and ginger ale, please."

Jolene gave him a sympathetic look. "All that trouble in the parking lot messed up your stomach, hasn't it? How about a little oatmeal on the side? Oatmeal might help settle you some, too."

Miles looked slightly more cheerful at the prospect of oatmeal. "That would be great, thank you."

Jolene nodded and strode away to put the order in.

"That was nice of her," said Myrtle cheerfully. She looked over at the door and said, "Gracious, look who's coming in."

Miles turned as unobtrusively as he could. Cash Baxter, Palmer's husband, was striding into the diner. He was wearing an expensive-looking suit and looked, as always, very well-groomed.

Red's hassled-looking deputy, Tucker, said, "If you could just stay here in the diner for a few minutes until the police chief can speak with you. Sorry, but the state police are just pulling in and it's going to be a busy few minutes."

Before Cash could say anything in return, the deputy scuttled outside again.

Cash gave a very irritated sigh and glanced around the diner with disinterest. A moment later, a *very* senior citizen called out to him. "Yoo-hoo!"

He pasted a smile on his face and walked over. "It's . . . Miss Myrtle, isn't it?"

Cash held out his hand for the handshake far before he could reach Myrtle's hand, which she recognized as a country club type of shake. She daintily took his hand and then said, "Do you know my friend, Miles?"

The handshake Cash offered Miles was quite a bit stronger than the one he offered Myrtle, judging by the expression on Miles's face.

Myrtle said, "Won't you sit down and join us? You must be needing a seat, surely. What horrible, horrible news."

A somber look passed over Cash's features. "Yes," he said slowly as he sat next to Miles. "Yes, it's come as a terrible shock. You know, then. Well, I guess you must have heard from your son just now."

Myrtle shook her head. "I'm afraid Miles and I came across Palmer when we were about to go into the diner. We're so very sorry."

Miles nodded in agreement and Cash sighed again, running a hand through his formerly-immaculately brushed hair. He seemed, actually, rather nervous. His gaze darted around the restaurant, almost as if he were looking for someone.

Miles cleared his throat. "They're not technically open, but they've been kind enough to serve Myrtle and me. I'm sure they'll do the same for you."

Cash gave him a tight smile. "Thanks. Yes, I might need to have a little something. I feel—well, I suppose I must be in shock. It hasn't hit me yet."

Myrtle supposed that might be why Cash seemed remarkably unperturbed by Palmer's sudden demise. "You look as if you might have been about to head away on a business trip of some kind. I do believe Palmer said you traveled quite a bit."

Cash nodded absently. "Yes. Unfortunately, that comes with the territory. My red-eye flight from Tucson came in an hour ago and I'd just arrived home when Red's deputy approached me. He was clearly wanting me to stay at home, but I'm not one to hang around and wait. I like to try and *do* things. Get information, make things happen. Fix problems."

Myrtle said, "I'm sure those are very good qualities to have in business. Miles, didn't those traits come in helpful when you were an analyst?"

"Engineer," Miles gritted through his teeth.

Cash looked at Miles with new respect. "Yes, I'm sure they would have come in handy for an engineer. At any rate, I'm here. And since I'm not getting any information from the police, I'd appreciate the two of you filling me in."

Myrtle gazed sadly at him. "It was so very tragic. Miles parked his car—it's the black sedan out there—and walked away to see what the hours were on the door of the diner since we couldn't recall. While he was gone, I looked around the parking lot and noticed the truck and that the driver's side door was open. When I walked over to take a look, I discovered poor Palmer."

Cash's lips tightened and he swallowed. "I see. Could you tell what had happened to her? Was it a natural death?"

"I'm afraid it was a most unnatural one. However, I'm quite sure she didn't feel a thing. She appeared to be focused on something in her front seat when it happened."

Cash asked, "Did you have a chance to see what it was in her front seat?"

Myrtle blinked innocently at him. "It was only an impression, you understand, but it seemed to be a notebook."

"Was it?" asked Cash in that absent way of his again.

Myrtle nodded. Then she decided to ask a question of her own in her sweetest old lady voice. "Miles and I get up dreadfully early, don't we, Miles?"

Miles, who had been looking as if he might be about to nod off, despite the coffee, quickly straightened up and agreed.

"For me, it's that I can usually *fall* asleep, but I can't stay asleep. Lately, I've been getting up for the day around three or four every morning. It's not really *ideal*, but it's much better because Miles doesn't sleep either. I'll toddle down to his house and we'll put on some coffee and eat a bit. This morning, we watched nature documentaries."

Miles gave her a look that indicated he still considered it was something of a betrayal that Myrtle had slept during them.

Cash was looking longingly at the door as if he wanted very badly to escape this verbal sleep diary of Myrtle's. He strained to keep a polite smile on his face.

"The thing is, Cash, I was wondering if Palmer was the same way. Was it completely *normal* for Palmer to be out so early at the diner?"

Suddenly, Cash looked rather flustered. This was, in fact, the first time he'd looked flustered throughout the entire unusual event. His face was a blotchy red. He seemed to be about to say something when a voice came from behind them.

"Would Palmer have been at the diner so early because of *this*?"

They turned to see Red standing there holding the notebook.

It was then that Miles and Myrtle's food arrived.

"Can I get you something, too, sugar?" Jolene asked Cash in between gum chewing.

He hesitated. "Actually, could I just get some black coffee? And maybe an order of oatmeal?"

He seemed to have been inspired by Miles's insipid meal. Then he turned reluctantly to Red.

Red said, "How about if you and I speak outside?"

# Chapter Six

Cash, however, seemed quite reluctant to speak with Red alone. He hesitated again and said, "Do you mind if we talk right here, Red? Like I said, I'm pretty worn out from my red-eye flight."

Red shrugged, although Myrtle could tell he was irritated. He pulled up a chair to the side of the booth and set the notebook down. Gesturing at it, Red asked in a low voice, "Do you know much about your wife's plans for purchasing the diner?"

"Not very much, no. Of course, she talked about it briefly with me. Although I didn't know she specifically meant the diner. She'd mentioned purchasing a local business and I encouraged her."

His tone was matter-of-fact except for a slight note of disdain or condescension that Myrtle picked up on. She was sure it wouldn't go down well with Red.

Sure enough, Red sounded a bit aggravated when he said, "Was this an everyday thing? I think if my wife mentioned buying a business, I'm pretty sure I'd remember everything about it."

"I didn't realize she was far enough along to propose a sale. Is that what Palmer was doing here?" Cash's shoulders relaxed in relief.

"You tell me," said Red.

Cash paused and said slowly, "May I see the notebook?"

Red pushed it closer to him and Cash carefully skimmed several pages. "I see. Palmer had a well-thought-out proposal here. A slight change of name for the venue, revamping the menu and interior of the diner."

Red said, "And she was apparently planning on letting the staff go. At least, that's what's in her notes."

"It would have been a very different venue. Sometimes a business needs to pivot and hire new staff to better suit a new enterprise."

Myrtle could tell that Red didn't care much for Cash's professorial tone. His lips pressed together.

At that point, Lieutenant Perkins with the state police came in the door. Myrtle waved him over. "Lieutenant Perkins! I'd hoped you'd be the one to come over."

"It's good to see you, Mrs. Clover. You too, Mr. Bradford." He gave Cash a somber look. "Sir, let me extend my condolences."

Cash looked relieved to see him. "Thank you. And thank you for coming to Bradley to oversee the investigation."

This statement pleased Red even less. In fact, his face was starting to match his red hair. It was clear to him that Cash, relatively new to town, considered Red a bumbling local cop.

Even Myrtle was starting to feel defensive on Red's behalf. Miles, now feeling uncomfortable from the tension, unhappily stirred his oatmeal as he stared into the bowl.

Jolene, oblivious to the tension, slid a cup of black coffee in front of Cash.

Perkins picked up on Cash's subtext quickly and said, "Oh, I'm just here to lend a hand. Mostly the state police are here for support and to provide equipment and tools a local police department might not have."

Before Cash could respond, and it looked very much as if he was going to continue in the same vein, Perkins smoothly added,

"Red and I were wondering if you could go ahead and provide us with a statement so we can begin our search for the perpetrator."

Cash nodded. "Of course. I'm happy to help out."

Red said, "You mentioned a red-eye flight. Can you tell us a little more about your trip and when you arrived back in town?"

"Yes, I was away in Tucson for a few nights. I came back to the Charlotte airport very early this morning and then drove over to Bradley. I'd just gotten home when your deputy showed up at the house."

Red said, "Were you surprised to discover that your wife wasn't there?"

A flash of irritation crossed Cash's handsome features. "I wouldn't say *surprised*. I certainly took note of it, of course. I don't know if you knew Palmer at all, but she's . . . was . . . a very busy woman. She was on just about every committee and in every organization in town. Sometimes she would have a particularly frantic day ahead of her and she'd set out early for a run. Palmer took care of herself and always wanted to make sure she fit her exercise in before anything else."

Yet another annoying trait of Palmer's, reflected Myrtle.

Perkins said, "How had Palmer been lately? Can you tell us anything about her state of mind? Was she worried about anything?"

Cash's voice was solemn. "She was happy. She liked Bradley and the people she got to know. Our marriage was one for the ages. Palmer had so many gifts that it's criminal, literally, for them to go unexploited. She and I weren't ones to argue. We had a partnership in every way."

Red tilted his head to one side. "Your wife didn't mention having any problems with anyone in town? She hadn't had any run-ins with anyone?"

Cash gave him a chilly glare. "Of course not. Palmer wasn't one to engage in petty disputes. Her eye was always on the big picture. I will say that sometimes people may not have *understood* Palmer. She was so focused, so driven, so passionate. People just didn't *get* her. In a small town like this one, those feelings might have translated into jealousy."

Perkins asked, "Was there anyone in particular that you think might have been jealous?"

Cash was quiet for a moment. Then he shook his head. "No one in particular, no. Although, now that I think about it, there was someone who might have been upset with Palmer. Completely *unreasonably* upset with Palmer, I might add."

Perkins waited patiently for Cash to continue. Red appeared even more annoyed than he had before.

Finally, Cash said, "There's a woman named Nancy that Palmer was helping out. That's something else about Palmer—she was very generous to those in need. We have her cousin, Shay, living in a house on our property, as a matter of fact. Anyway, Nancy was in desperate straits, from what Palmer had told me."

"Does Nancy have a last name?" drawled Red.

Cash frowned, whether in an effort to remember the elusive last name or whether at Red's tone, it wasn't clear. He said, "I'm not sure Palmer ever mentioned it to me. But there couldn't be too many Nancys in town. This particular Nancy borrowed money from Palmer to help keep her utilities on and whatnot.

Palmer is very businesslike with those sorts of transactions." He sighed and corrected himself. "Palmer *was*, I mean. She asked Nancy several times to pay her back—Palmer had a signed contract and everything. But Nancy wouldn't."

Perkins asked, "Wouldn't? Or couldn't?"

Cash shrugged. "Either way. Palmer didn't appreciate being treated like an ATM. She'd very carefully created a repayment schedule with Nancy with Nancy's own bills and income in mind. So she found it very upsetting when Nancy didn't pay when she was supposed to."

"Did Palmer often lend people money?" asked Red.

"I don't think it was an everyday occurrence, but it happened relatively often both here and in Texas. People knew Palmer was generous."

"And wealthy," added Red.

"Yes, I suppose they did," Cash acquiesced. "But she wouldn't have stayed that way if she just gave away money without any plans on getting it back. If she didn't get repayment, she wouldn't lend again to that person."

Perkins asked, "Do you think Nancy would have been upset enough to have done something like this?"

Cash held out his hands. "I have absolutely no idea. But you asked for names of people who might have held a grudge against Palmer and she came to mind."

The door to the diner opened and a young woman wearing a waitress uniform came through. She stopped, looking startled at the sight of Red and Perkins at the booth and quickly scuttled to the kitchen.

Red said, "I guess that's all I've got. Anything else from you, Perkins?"

Perkins shook his head and gave Cash a smile. "Unfortunately, even if we find out any information, we're not going to be able to disclose it. I know you must be exhausted from your flight in this morning—you should head back home."

There was a crash as if a pile of plates had been dropped and then the sound of Bo fussing at someone.

"I think we're throwing them off their game in the kitchen," said Red dryly as he stood up and headed out the door with Perkins.

Cash drained his coffee and said slowly, "I suppose I might as well go."

Myrtle said, "I can tell you from past experience that Red is very tight-lipped about his cases. I'm afraid he's not likely to share anything he finds out."

Cash frowned but appeared to be resigned to that fact. He stood up, gave them a polite goodbye, and headed out.

"This place is wild today," said Myrtle.

"Like Red said, we're probably messing them up by being here so early. They're having a tough time juggling customers and prep work at the same time," said Miles.

"Such a tough time that they're breaking down in tears?" asked Myrtle, lifting her eyebrows.

Sure enough, the young waitress who'd just come in was crying, running her mascara, as she refilled the ketchup bottles on the tables. When she reached Myrtle and Miles, she asked in a cracking voice, "Y'all need a refill of ketchup?"

Realizing the young woman probably could barely see through her tears, Myrtle said, "I'm sure the ketchup bottle is fine. I've already eaten my food and Miles certainly doesn't need any ketchup with his oatmeal. Why don't you have a seat, Mariah?"

Mariah hesitated, looking toward the kitchen. Then she sat down in the chair that Red had pulled over to the booth. "Thanks, Miss Myrtle."

Myrtle pushed an unused water glass over to her. "Here, this water hasn't been touched. And here are some tissues." She pulled a Kleenex packet out of her voluminous purse and slid it over to her.

Mariah obediently sipped the water and swabbed at her face with the tissues. She was an attractive young woman with high cheekbones, large blue eyes, and shoulder-length blonde hair that she had pulled back in a ponytail.

"Feeling better?" asked Myrtle.

Mariah sighed. "A little. But it's not normal to have a body in the parking lot."

"No, of course it's not. But the police are there, and they'll figure out who did this, don't you worry."

However, Myrtle's confident statement seemed to have the opposite effect on Mariah. She now seemed even more concerned than she had previously.

Miles cleared his throat, "Did you know Palmer Baxter?"

Myrtle frowned at him. She preferred that her sidekicks be seen and not heard.

The young woman quickly shook her head. "No. I mean, I recognized the truck and I've seen her around town, but I didn't *know* her."

Myrtle tapped her finger on the Formica table. "I understand that Palmer had plans to purchase this diner. It sounds like she'd wanted to change it into a café of some sort, complete with new staff."

The young woman said, "That's true. She was in here a couple of times, pretty early. I heard her talking with Bo. He's the owner, you know."

Miles said, "I'm guessing Bo wasn't interested in selling the diner."

"Not at all," said Mariah. "To him, it's like a family legacy. His grandfather started the diner ages ago. They passed the name Bo down to the oldest son. It's living history, he's always saying."

Myrtle considered this. "So, when Bo was telling Palmer that he wasn't interested in selling, I'm guessing she didn't completely accept that."

The young woman shook her head. "I guess she wasn't used to having people tell her no. Palmer was mad, that's for sure. He'd tell her over and over that he didn't want to sell and she kept pushing him. I could tell she was really mad." Tears welled up in her eyes and she grabbed another tissue. "But now she's gone. It's hard to believe she was just here and now she's . . . dead."

She glanced over at the kitchen and saw one of her coworkers glaring at her. "I'd better go. Thanks for letting me have a seat for a second."

Myrtle looked thoughtful as Mariah scurried back to work with the ketchup bottles.

"I think we should leave, Myrtle," said Miles evenly. "We've finished eating and we're probably in their way right before they open."

Myrtle nodded absently, giving him some carefully-folded dollar bills for her meal and a tip. He walked to the front counter and paid and then they walked outside.

# Chapter Seven

"I think we're going to have to walk home. The crime scene tape surrounds the whole area where my car is," said Miles.

"It's not far. Besides, maybe it's a good idea to walk off the food we just ate." They set out, away from the flashing lights of the emergency vehicles in the background.

"What did you make of all that?" asked Myrtle.

"Well, obviously someone wasn't happy with Palmer. But from what I saw at the book club meeting, she doesn't seem like the easiest person to get along with. Unfortunately, I have the feeling that Bo is going to end up as one of Red's suspects."

Myrtle snorted. "Maybe Bo will be one of Lieutenant *Perkins's* suspects. But it was completely obvious that Red has latched onto Cash. Could you tell that Red didn't like him one bit? He just couldn't stand him."

Miles jumped suddenly and Myrtle frowned at him. "What's wrong with you?"

He glanced down and Pasha, Myrtle's black cat, was smiling up at him enigmatically.

"Brilliant Pasha! You're keeping Miles and me company," said Myrtle, beaming at the animal.

"She wanted to give me a fright," muttered Miles.

"Don't be silly. Pasha doesn't have underlying motives. You're attributing human foibles to the poor creature. There's a word for that: anthropomorphism."

Pasha bumped her head lovingly against Myrtle while giving Miles a mocking look.

Miles's face indicated that he was not convinced. "I believe she thinks it's funny."

"That's completely absurd." Myrtle reached down to stroke the cat and she gave Myrtle a conspiratorial look.

"What were we talking about?" asked Myrtle as they continued on their way with Pasha now joining them.

"No idea," said Miles, sounding rather sulky.

"Oh, I remember. Red's reaction to Cash."

Pasha brushed up against Miles's leg again and he looked anxiously down at her. Pasha, as a feral cat, could be unpredictable. Pasha smiled up at him again.

"Pay attention, Miles!" said Myrtle. "Sidekicks are supposed to be attentive."

Miles dragged his focus away from Pasha and her mysterious Mona Lisa smile.

Myrtle continued, "Cash was fairly dismissive of Red. I got the impression that he thought Red might be the stereotypical bumbling rural cop. It actually made me bristle. I felt very much like a mama bear." She considered this unusual feeling.

Miles said, "Well, that's natural, isn't it? Red might annoy you, but he's very good at his job. The town would get rid of him if he weren't. He handles a variety of different types of calls and resolves them all."

Myrtle nodded. "He does do a good job. I could tell Cash's attitude got under Red's skin

"But Myrtle, even if Red has pegged Cash for the murder, it doesn't sound as if he'll be able to prove it in court. Cash was apparently on a very early flight or driving from the airport to Bradley when the crime occurred."

Pasha bumped up against Miles's leg and Miles frowned down at the cat again.

"That remains to be seen," said Myrtle. "His alibi is going to have to be checked out; and I'm sure it will be. Obviously, the spouse is the most-likely suspect with these types of murders."

They reached Myrtle's house, a fact which Miles was most thankful over. Pasha bounded in the door in front of them.

"Let me get you some fresh water," said Myrtle.

Miles said, "That would be great. It was hotter outside than I realized."

"I was talking to Pasha, actually. The poor dear is wearing a fur coat, you know. But I'll get glasses for you and me, too. You'd do a lot better if you dressed for the weather, Miles."

"Old habits die hard," said Miles, looking down at his usual outfit of khaki pants and a button-down shirt over a white undershirt.

Pasha eagerly lapped up a good deal of the water and then sat in a corner of the living room where she kept an eye on Miles. And Miles kept an eye on her.

Myrtle said, "What did you make of the fact that Palmer was planning on purchasing the diner?"

Miles took a big sip of water. He then said, "I thought it was a bad business idea. The diner is a beloved fixture in the town and very busy. Plus, people here don't like or appreciate or even adapt to change. I don't think a café with fluffy curtains and fancy menu was going to go over very well."

"It certainly wouldn't have. I could have told her that. Of course, Palmer did seem like the kind of person who had her own opinions. I'm not sure she would have listened if someone had tried to advise her on it."

Miles said in a musing tone, "Mariah made it sound as if Palmer was being very pushy about it."

"Well, she couldn't have bought it if Bo hadn't sold it to her. And, apparently, he wasn't interested."

Miles was still ruminating on the business side of the scuttled transaction. "The whole thing had disaster written all over it. From what I understand, Palmer had no experience in the restaurant industry."

"The disaster is what happened in the parking lot this morning. I have to wonder if it's not somehow tied into the Bo's Diner proposed sale."

Miles frowned. "You're not saying you think Bo had anything to do with Palmer's death? I don't think anyone in Bradley would thank you if the diner had to close down because Bo was dragged off to prison."

"If he did it, he'll have to pay the consequences. But no, I doubt he did. He's never seemed the hot-tempered type to me. You never know, though—Palmer might have been so pushy and obnoxious that he lost it. Or maybe a server or cook was worried about losing his job because of a potential sale. Her notes did indicate that Palmer wasn't planning on transferring over any of the staff."

Miles said, "Resorting to murder smacks of more desperation than someone facing a career change. I don't know, Myrtle. We might need to look in another direction."

"The problem is that you and I didn't know Palmer very well."

Miles said, "From what I know of Palmer, I'm not convinced that was a problem. It sounds more like we had a lucky escape."

"But we don't really understand who might have been upset enough with Palmer to do her in."

Miles said, "I guess we have that one lead that Cash mentioned. The woman Palmer loaned money to. What did you make of all that?"

Myrtle sniffed. "It sounded a lot like Palmer, didn't it? It's not as if she's doing any of her good deeds out of a sense of compassion. She has other motivations."

"Attention?"

"Definitely," said Myrtle. "And perhaps to make herself feel good or important. So when she loaned Nancy money, she definitely wanted it back and in a particular timeframe. I'm almost surprised she didn't attach terms of interest to the transaction."

"Cash claimed that Palmer set things up that way because she was very businesslike about her lending."

Myrtle said, "It would have been kinder for her to have just sent Nancy off to the bank if she was planning on hounding Nancy if she didn't pay on schedule."

Miles was quiet for a moment. "It seems sort of rash of this Nancy to have killed Palmer just because she was being pushy about getting her money back."

Myrtle shrugged. "That might not have been the full story. We'll have to go talk with her."

"Do you know which Nancy it is?"

Myrtle said, "I have a pretty good idea. But she's not the first person I want to speak with. You and I need to go present Shay Cunningham with a sympathy casserole."

Miles drew back in his chair. "Who are we doing this to?"

Myrtle frowned at him. "What an odd way to put it, Miles. We're not *inflicting* a casserole on Shay. We're *bestowing* it on her. She'll be an appreciative recipient."

Miles looked less-than-convinced. "I don't know who Shay is."

"She's the woman who lives in the cottage behind Cash and Palmer. She's Palmer's cousin."

"Oh, right. The poor cousin that Palmer took in."

Myrtle said, "I'm sure Palmer bragged about her charitable action plenty of times. Poor cousin, indeed. Anyway, we'll go and see her later today, bearing a casserole."

Miles's expression seemed to indicate he wasn't sure this was the best of ideas.

"What's wrong now, Miles? Heavens, but you're in an obstructive mood today."

Miles said, "Won't Shay be questioned by the police today? I would think they'd be all over Palmer's property looking for clues as to why someone would want to kill her."

"They won't be there *all* day. Besides, they wouldn't be searching Shay's cottage unless they have a search warrant. And currently, I can't imagine why Shay would want to murder Palmer. From everything we understand, Palmer was the one thing that stood between Shay and homelessness."

Miles said, "Perhaps we should purchase food and bring it over. We could pick up lunch from Bo's Diner for Shay, for instance."

Myrtle scowled at him. "Picking up food from a restaurant doesn't convey the same level of sympathy as a homemade meal."

"I'm sure Shay would appreciate it," said Miles fervently.

But Myrtle already had plans of her own. "I have an old recipe book of my mother's. There's a casserole in there that will be perfect. I have all the ingredients for it, too. Well, aside from fresh chicken. But there's no reason I can't use canned."

Miles was starting to look very unhappy.

Myrtle knit her brows. "There's also the matter of mayo. But I can substitute salad dressing. That's pretty much all Ranch dressing is—mayonnaise."

Miles quickly said, "I can run by my house and bring mayo by. I have some."

"No, no. There's no need for that. Cooking is meant to be a creative endeavor. And right now, I feel very inspired."

"One important aspect of cooking is to *taste* the concoction you're making," Miles pointed out helpfully.

But Myrtle didn't appear to be listening. Instead, she was already heading into the kitchen for her mother's cookbook which, when she pulled it out, appeared to be well over a hundred years old. Pasha trotted into the kitchen to watch her with interest.

Myrtle opened the old book, which was barely holding itself together. She ran her finger down the table of contents until she got to the section she was looking for. Then she frowned. "Hm. Maybe there are more ingredients I don't have."

Miles looked relieved. "That sounds like a sign that we should go to Bo's Diner, as I mentioned."

Myrtle said absently, "Tippy had some wonderful braised brisket at her last do."

"Tippy has a staff and you don't. Plus, comfort food might be best. Like hot dogs and hamburgers from Bo's Diner."

"You're starting to sound like a broken record, Miles."

"I'm just trying to think of what might be easiest," said Miles, looking uneasy as he often did when fibbing.

Myrtle put her ancient cookbook aside and pondered the problem. Then she said slowly, "You know, Puddin was bragging a few weeks ago."

"Sounds likely. I've heard about her recent Myrtle Beach vacation at least twice and she's not even my housekeeper."

"She was saying," said Myrtle, "that she had cooked an amazing chicken and dumplings meal."

"I'm not certain we can count on Puddin to be completely truthful."

"No. But I'm not much in the mood for going to the grocery store right now and there's only so much creativity that's allowed in the parameters of a recipe."

Miles looked reassured to hear this acknowledged.

"Plus, Puddin might have information on Palmer. You know what a gossip-monger she is. She seemed to have plenty of opinions about her. Maybe I can find out what direction we should be going in to find out more."

Miles raised his eyebrows. "That sounds more like the underlying reason you want her over here. I was wondering why you might want to inflict Puddin on yourself again."

"I'll call her up now." Myrtle reached for her phone.

"I'll see you later, then, Myrtle," said Miles as he walked toward the door.

"Just a little while later. We'll run over to Shay's cottage after the meal is ready. This afternoon."

"If I'm able to retrieve my car by then," said Miles. "It's still at the diner.

"I'm sure the police will free it up soon."

Miles sighed and slipped out the door.

At first, it was a little challenging to even get Puddin on the phone. Dusty appeared to be screening calls for her. Myrtle finally, in frustration, said, "Dusty, I want Puddin to cook a meal for me. I'll give her money for the ingredients and whatnot. I heard about her legendary chicken pot pie."

Dusty paused as if surprised to hear this.

Myrtle frowned. "Puddin *is* a good cook, isn't she? I haven't been misled?"

Dusty gave a non-committal grunt as if he didn't want to offend the cook.

Suddenly, Dusty was gone and Puddin was on the phone with her. Myrtle could imagine the smirk on her face as she said, "Want me to cook, huh?"

"Not as a regular thing. Just this one time. I was all set to cook a recipe but then it seemed I didn't have any of the ingredients. I don't feel like going to the grocery store, either. If you can run by the store to pick up whatever you need for the recipe, I'll pay you back."

"And you'll pay me for cooking," said Puddin in the tone of someone wanting to make sure of all the facts before entering an agreement.

"Of course I will. But you're not exactly an executive chef and I'm not exactly a rich person. The pay would be commiserated with the task and the outcome."

Puddin muttered, "Don't like it when you don't speak English."

"Just run by the store on your way over. See you in a bit."

# Chapter Eight

Surprisingly, Puddin was over at Myrtle's house just thirty minutes later. Myrtle discovered why when Puddin said, "Bitsy says you found Palmer Baxter dead."

Bitsy was Puddin's cousin. She was also a housekeeper but a new-and-improved version of Puddin. Her services, however, were much in demand and far too expensive for someone on a limited retirement income.

"Indeed I did. That's why I need you to go ahead and work on this food. I'm going to be taking it over to Palmer's cousin this morning."

Puddin pulled things out of her grocery bags as she considered this. The recipe seemed to involve a rotisserie chicken and canned biscuits. "Bitsy knew Palmer, you know. Cleaned for her."

"That doesn't surprise me."

Puddin pulled an aluminum container out of the bag and Myrtle stopped her. "You can use one of my Corning Ware dishes."

Puddin scowled at her. "Then you'll have to go back and get it after they're done eatin'."

"Precisely," said Myrtle. Puddin continued scowling and Myrtle said, "Don't worry—I'll pay you for the aluminum container."

This settled, Puddin continued with her tales of Bitsy's adventures in housekeeping. "Bitsy says Palmer's house is *huge*. They hafta pay her a ton to clean it. Lots of expensive stuff in there, too." Puddin glanced around at Myrtle's meager possessions scornfully.

"Sounds like a house that's so big it's become a problem," said Myrtle. She was very satisfied with her small space.

Puddin looked miffed that Myrtle wasn't as impressed with her story as she wanted her to be. This usually meant that she was going to amp up the narrative to make her audience more appreciative.

"That ain't all," she said, lowering her voice as if perhaps the neighbors could hear her through the walls. "Bitsy says she's havin' an *affair*."

This was news indeed. Myrtle frowned. "That's actually very important information, Puddin."

Puddin looked pleased.

"You need to tell Red about it," continued Myrtle.

Puddin recoiled a little. "Nope. I don't know nothin' else about it."

"Well then, tell Bitsy to talk to Red about it. If Palmer was having an affair, that means there's someone out there with a motive. Did Bitsy say who it was that Palmer was having this illicit relationship with?"

Puddin shook her head sullenly.

Myrtle said, "I may want to have a conversation with Bitsy. She's always seemed to be the kind of person who has her head screwed on right. If Palmer was having an affair, Bitsy could well have picked up on that."

Puddin looked very unenthusiastic about any of this. "Bitsy might get fired by Palmer's husband or somethin.'"

"Then he's not worth working for. Besides, Bitsy has plenty of other paying clients. She'd probably appreciate having some extra time in her schedule to breathe. Speaking of time, Puddin, that chicken and dumplings isn't going to cook itself, you know."

Puddin, in a much worse mood than she was when she started, continued assembling the meal. She cast a wary eye at Pasha, who'd come strolling in to watch the proceedings.

"Keep that witch-cat away from me."

"Pasha has *no* interest in you, Puddin. She's all about that rotisserie chicken you've brought in."

Pasha's eyes gleamed as Puddin removed the top from the container.

"How long is this going to take to cook?"

Puddin shrugged. "Just about thirty minutes."

"Excellent. I think I should take it over there warm. So I'll be over there a bit earlier than I thought I would be." Myrtle made to head back out to the living room but Puddin stopped her.

"Hey, I wanna hear what happened this morning!" protested Puddin.

"*That's* why you were so eager to come over here this morning. I thought so. You just want some gossip. Gossip is your stock in trade, isn't it? Your currency?"

Puddin glared at her, eyes small in her pale face. "English!"

"What I'm speaking is a good deal more similar to English than what you're spewing out."

Puddin continued glaring at her.

Myrtle sighed. "All right, I'll toss you a bone. Miles and I were at the diner early. Palmer was there, too. We found her—dead."

Puddin said, "In the diner?" The expression on her face indicated that she was going to have to find another place to eat out if this were true.

"No, in the parking lot. She'd been struck on the head from behind." Myrtle pursed her lips. "A terrible business. And that, *really*, is all I know."

Or all she was prepared to share with Puddin.

Puddin was true to her word for once and the chicken and dumplings was ready to go just thirty minutes later. Puddin showed every indication of wanting to stay at Myrtle's house to eat her snacks and watch game shows. Myrtle, however, was successful at herding her out.

Then she called Miles. "It's all ready."

Miles sounded very much as if he might have been napping. "Hmm?"

"The meal for Shay."

Miles was very slow to catch on. "Shay."

"Yes. For heaven's sake, Miles. We're going to see Palmer's poor cousin Shay and present her with chicken and dumplings. That must have been some nap you took."

Miles was still trying to shake off the vestiges of sleep. "And the food is okay?"

"Well, it smells good. Puddin seemed pleased with it. The main thing is that I didn't have to go to the store. Come on, let's go see Shay before the food is cold."

"I'll be by in a few," said Miles before getting off the phone.

But it ended up being a bit more than a few. Miles finally showed up at her door about thirty minutes later. Myrtle had been tapping her foot.

"I had to reclaim my car," he said simply.

"Ah. I'd forgotten about it. Glad the police were able to let it go."

They climbed into Miles's car and headed off for the Baxter estate.

"Where is this?" asked Miles.

"It's that tremendous house on the lake."

"There are quite a few of them," pointed out Miles helpfully.

Myrtle said, "This is the one that's really over-the-top. It's like the architect was on drugs or something."

Miles shook his head. "I don't know it."

"Would you like me to drive?" asked Myrtle impatiently.

Miles decidedly did not. He'd gotten rather protective of his car lately. "Just direct me over there."

Myrtle got them over to the house. It was a rambling monstrosity that had clearly had wings added to it over time. The house faced the lake, so they were driving up to the back.

"Where's Shay's cottage?" asked Miles, glancing around.

Myrtle peered through the windshield and out the windows. "I think it must be that building over there."

"That? I thought that was a storage shed for the yard equipment or something."

"People like this have a yard service, Miles. Even *I* have a yard service and I'm not 'people like this.'"

Miles looked at her thoughtfully. "How long have you had Dusty working for you? Just out of curiosity."

"Mercy. I suppose it's been ten years now."

Miles frowned. "You were doing your own yardwork before then? In your seventies?"

"No, that's what hale and hearty sons are for. Red took care of it. He just zipped across the street with his riding mower after he'd finished with his own lawn. Did the bushes, too."

Miles said, "I'm surprised you stopped that arrangement. I'm sure Red was more reliable than Dusty is."

"He was. But Red also seemed to think that doing my yard-work meant it gave him the privilege to offer me his opinion on a variety of different topics. I was spending entirely too much time with Red." Myrtle glanced impatiently across the expanse of the Baxter estate. "Let's head over to that storage shed or what-have-you."

Driving up, they discovered there was more to the shed than met the eye. Although very modest at the front, the back of the cottage extended fairly far.

"This might even be a two-bedroom house," said Miles.

"Yes, I think it is. It's not all that close to the main house, is it? I suppose Palmer didn't mind being generous as long as she didn't have to see the beneficiary."

Myrtle picked up the chicken and dumplings and they climbed out of Miles's car and walked over to the cottage.

"No police here right now," said Miles, sounding relieved.

"I suppose they're probably more interested in the big house. Maybe Red is still working on getting a warrant to search it."

Myrtle knocked at the door and it opened after a minute to reveal a rather faded-looking woman with a careworn face. Myrtle figured she must have been in her thirties, but she looked much older.

"Miss Myrtle," said Shay, smiling at her. "What a nice surprise."

Myrtle said briskly, "I heard the news about Palmer and wanted to do something, dear. I've brought along my friend, Miles. Do you know Miles?"

Shay apparently didn't because she reached out a hand and shook his. "It's a pleasure. Won't the two of you come in?"

They followed her into a very tidy home. Shay didn't have a lot of things, but what she did have was carefully put in its place. The cottage was dimly-lit because of the heavy shading from the pine trees outside. But Shay had clearly tried to make it as cheerful as possible. The walls were painted a cheery yellow and the furniture and rug were all in bright shades.

"What a beautiful place," said Myrtle. "Did you decorate yourself or was the house like this when you arrived?"

Shay smiled at her, looking pleased. "Thank you, Miss Myrtle. I decorated it myself, over time. I just kept heading over to the thrift shop to see what they'd gotten in. I lucked out with the furniture I was able to find."

Myrtle said, "Here's a little something for you to enjoy later." She handed over the grocery bag which had the chicken and dumplings container settled in the bottom.

A slight wariness descended over Shay's features. Myrtle's cooking was legendary. Miles quickly said, "It's Puddin's famous chicken and dumplings." Shay's expression cleared and she said, "That's so kind of you! Let me put this in the fridge real quick."

Myrtle scowled at Miles. She'd been planning on taking credit for the dish, herself.

Miles said mildly, "Just giving credit where credit is due."

Shay returned to the little living room and said, "I appreciate the two of you dropping by. I haven't been able to believe the news today. It just doesn't seem real to me." She paused, her brow crinkling. "Actually, do I remember right? Did the two of you find poor Palmer this morning?"

Myrtle nodded somberly. "I'm afraid so."

"Oh, how awful for you!" Shay shuddered. "I'd have nightmares if it were me. Just awful. What a way for Palmer to go. She'd been so good to me. She saved my life, you know."

Myrtle just nodded sympathetically. She was hoping Shay would elaborate, which she eventually did, mostly to fill in the silence.

"I was having a terrible time of it. My life was full of toil and worry."

Myrtle saw Miles quirk an eyebrow very slightly at Shay's rather dramatic, Victorian wording.

"My family perished in an automobile accident. I took to drinking." Here Shay hung her head. "I guess I was just trying to drown my sorrows or something. The only problem was that I couldn't hold down a job with the kind of drinking I was doing."

"Oversleeping, Shay?" asked Myrtle, the very picture of care and concern.

Shay nodded, giving Myrtle a shy smile. "Oversleeping. But when I woke up, I poured myself a drink to help wake up. Then I'd realize I was late for work and I'd pour myself another drink to make myself feel better. The only problem was that it made me feel better, *much* better for a little while, but then it didn't make me feel better after that."

"That all must have been very, very difficult," said Myrtle.

Shay gave a big sigh. "It was. Mostly because I lost my job and couldn't get a reference for another one. Then, because I couldn't pay my rent, I lost the place I was renting. And, when you're kicked out of one place, it's like you have a black mark against your name. No one else wants to give you a lease. Plus, they'd ask for proof of income, and I didn't have any because I couldn't find a job."

Miles said slowly, "Did you become homeless, then?" He looked very troubled at the thought.

Shay nodded again. "I sure did. I was sleeping in my car for a while, at least until my car got repossessed because I couldn't make the payments. It was just one thing after another." Then she smiled. "But that's when Palmer found out what kind of situation I was in. I don't even know how she figured it out. I think she said she'd tried to reach me to send me an invitation to some kind of event or party she was having. Anyway, when she couldn't find my address, she dug deeper and learned about . . . everything. The next thing I knew, she'd driven over to Charlotte to find me and bring me here."

Myrtle said, "Did it take her long to figure out where you were?"

"It sure did. She asked the staff at the homeless shelters and people on the street if they'd seen me. She'd brought a picture of me and everything. I was just sitting on a bench near the park when Palmer found me. The next thing I knew, she was giving me a hug, bundling me into her car, and bringing me here." A single tear rolled down Shay's cheek. "She let me have this little place rent-free until I could get on my feet again."

Myrtle said, "It's a lovely home, Shay."

Shay smiled at her and then continued with the narrative. "Palmer was all set to send me to rehab, too, to help me out with my drinking problem. But when my money had run out, my drinking stopped, too. I had some bad days during that transition, but I'm all good now. So, like I said, Palmer saved me."

"What a wonderful thing for her to do, Shay. The two of you are cousins, I believe?"

"That's right. Our moms were sisters."

Myrtle had noticed that Palmer's husband hadn't figured into Shay's narrative so far and wondered how pleased he'd been about taking in Palmer's down-on-her-luck relative.

"Maybe so," said Shay. But she looked doubtful.

Miles cleared his throat. "Are we keeping you from work, Shay?"

Shay smiled at him and shook her head. "After the police came by, I took the day off. I knew I couldn't do anything but think about Palmer today. I'm glad the two of you came by. I think it's good for me to reminisce."

"Did the police come by very early this morning, then?" asked Myrtle.

"Before the sun had come up, yes. They woke me up, actually. I thought I was still sleeping and having a nightmare when they told me the news." She gave Myrtle a worried look. "Red seemed sort of suspicious of me."

"Oh, I'm sure he wasn't, dear. It's Red's job to be suspicious of everyone. Although I do think he takes it a little far sometimes. Why, he was probably suspicious of Miles and me for being on the scene the way we were."

This cheered Shay up a little. "Do you really think so?"

"Absolutely. Why on earth would you have wanted Palmer dead? It sounds as if she was supporting you."

Shay looked worried again. "He and that state policeman were asking a lot of questions about money."

"Were they? Palmer had a will, then, I'm guessing."

Shay said, "Palmer was always so responsible—with *everything*. Even though she was young and healthy, she had her will done, living will, the works. She even made Cash do it, too, even though I think he thought it was a waste of his time."

Miles asked curiously, "Did they have you go with them? To have your will drawn up, too?"

Shay shook her head ruefully. "They asked me about it, but the fact of the matter is that I don't have anything to leave behind. Just some second-hand furniture. I don't even have any savings to speak of. I never would ask Palmer for any money—she helped me out enough as it was. Any time any kind of unexpected expenses come up, I pay for them myself."

Miles said, "You have a job then? What do you do?"

Myrtle shot him a look that said that her sidekick needed to go into silent mode. She was far more interested in any will of Palmer's than what Shay did for a living.

But Shay was more than happy to elaborate on her job. She beamed at Miles. "I work at the animal shelter. I love the animals over there. Palmer helped me get the job. At first, I had no idea what I wanted to do for work. She asked me a ton of questions—she'd found some sort of questionnaire online that helped people figure out what they might be interested in. When she realized how much I loved animals, she found me my job."

Myrtle said quickly, "That's wonderful, Shay." She planned to launch into a few questions about Palmer's will.

Miles, however, had apparently missed Myrtle's reproving look and was still absorbed in Shay's job. "That seems like it might be a tough line of work for animal lovers, though. Don't you want to take all the dogs and cats home with you?" He glanced around the small cottage. "Unless they're hiding, I don't see any animals here."

Shay's features clouded up. "No, I don't bring them here—I just play with them at work and try to socialize them as much as possible. And, of course, I put out the word about them as much as possible." She looked hopefully at Miles. "Would you like a pet? There's Waggles who I've been trying to place for a while. He's a sweetheart."

Miles quickly shook his head. "I don't think I'm in the market for a pet right now."

Shay continued sadly, "Cash didn't want any animals in the cottage. Of course I respected that. They're already doing so much just lodging me here. I don't want to cause any issues."

Myrtle frowned. "Cash set the rules for the cottage? I'd gotten the impression that Palmer was the one holding the purse strings here. Wasn't she the owner of the house and property?"

"Well, I think it's a little complicated, you know. Marriages mean that everything sort of merges together. Palmer did buy the place outright. But Cash contributes income, too, of course.

I think he has a good job." Shay seemed a bit doubtful on this point.

"What is it he does again?" asked Myrtle.

Shay's doubt grew substantially at the question. "I'm not completely sure. Something he has to travel for. Sales? Computer stuff? I don't know."

Myrtle said, "Do you know much about Palmer's will? Did she provide for you in it?"

Shay nodded. "Cash was kind enough to come by and see me right after I found out. He wanted to let me know that, although most of Palmer's money went to Cash, she settled a small amount on me. He even gave me a copy of the will." Shay gestured vaguely to the coffee table, which had a neatly stapled set of documents on it.

Myrtle said, "Goodness, there it is?" She paused for a moment and then said, "Would you mind very much, dear, if I took a look at it? It's a terrible thing to ask, I know, but I've been thinking about revising my own will and this would help me figure out what direction I need to go in."

Miles raised his eyebrows at the impudence of the request. Or, perhaps, the fact he knew that Myrtle didn't have very much to leave to anyone and an elaborate will was definitely not required.

Shay quickly agreed, though, her eyes wide. She gestured to the document. "Of course you can. I'm awful with these things. Maybe you can make sense of it for me."

# Chapter Nine

Myrtle put on a pair of reading glasses and prepared to read the will with complete focus. This left a rather uncomfortable silence in the room. Miles smiled weakly at Shay who seemed to be desperately casting about in her mind for something to say.

Finally Shay said, "It was just too kind of you to bring food by."

Miles said, "It was our pleasure. Myrtle made all the arrangements. We were sorry to hear the news about Palmer. We just saw her yesterday, as a matter of fact. She was at our book club meeting."

"Oh, that's nice. I'm glad Palmer was able to have a fun day yesterday. Considering, well . . . "

Shay started crying in earnest now.

Myrtle shot Miles a look. The sidekick was decidedly not supposed to instigate any crying.

Myrtle said, "As far as the will goes, it looks like you're absolutely right, Shay. Palmer had most of her estate go to her husband, but she did settle a nice amount on you. And if Cash predeceases you, you'll be the sole beneficiary of the estate."

Shay blinked at this and gave an uneasy laugh. "I see. Well, that's not going to happen. Cash is in wonderful health. Palmer said he works out every day and even has a personal trainer. He'll live a nice, long life."

Myrtle said, "Miles and I saw Cash at the diner this morning, when the police were speaking with him."

Shay looked sad. "It must have been an awful shock for him."

"I'm sure it must have been, but he was holding up very well."

Shay said, "Are you married, Miss Myrtle? I feel like I should know, but I can't seem to remember."

Myrtle said, "Gracious, no. I've been a widow for longer than I was married. Being married was all well and good, but I wouldn't want to take on and train another man. Anyway, I was wondering about Palmer and Cash. What kind of marriage would you say they had?'

Shay seemed to take Myrtle's persistent nosiness in stride as something that came part and parcel with being very elderly. She said slowly, "It was very different, I think. Palmer always seemed in charge of everything. Cash always acted kind of . . . remote, I guess, when he was around Palmer. But he might just not be the kind of guy who shows a lot of emotion. There are people like that. Somehow, though, he and Palmer almost seemed more like roommates to me instead of a married couple."

Myrtle frowned. "Cash's manner did seem quite chilly to me yesterday morning. I thought maybe he was the kind of person who buried his feelings. Of course, anger is a very different kind of feeling and hard to bury. Did Cash ever show evidence of a temper? Did Palmer ever seem afraid of him in any way?"

Shay hesitated at this. "He usually seemed calm and controlled. But I did hear an awful argument between the two of them recently."

Myrtle just nodded, waiting patiently for Shay to elaborate. In a minute, she did. "It sounded to me like the argument was about money. I was outside their house, about to knock on the door because I was going to go to the grocery store and wanted to check and see if they needed anything."

Miles said, "So they didn't know you were there."

Shay flushed a little. "No. I kind of froze up because I didn't want them to think I was eavesdropping. But I guess I sort of was. Cash was wanting to buy something expensive and Palmer was really opposed to it. He wanted to purchase a bass boat. Palmer said that they already had a pontoon boat and he could fish off the side of that if he wanted to fish. But Cash said he'd look ridiculous fishing for bass off a pontoon boat. Palmer shut him down right away though and ended the conversation. Then I sneaked away and just went to the store without asking them if they wanted anything."

Myrtle said, "Do you know anything about where Palmer's money came from?"

Shay nodded. "It's all family money. Palmer's dad was a trader on Wall Street and she was his only child."

"He's no longer living?" asked Myrtle delicately.

"Palmer's father was in the same accident that killed my parents. Her mother was out of the picture right after Palmer was born so she wasn't part of her life at all."

"How awful about the accident," said Myrtle with a frown.

"I know. It wasn't long after Palmer and Cash got married." She took a deep breath and blinked fast at the thought of the accident. To Myrtle's relief, she was able to continue. "I'm not sure Palmer's dad was ever a huge fan of Cash's. I never understood why because he looked like he'd be the perfect husband. He had a good job, always seemed respectful of Palmer, and was handsome, to boot." She shrugged. "I guess I understood more after I moved in."

"Because of how distant he is?" asked Miles.

"Right. He's just not a very warm person." Shay sighed. "Still, I know he's going to be so heartbroken over Palmer's death. I should go over and speak with him."

Myrtle and Miles stood up. "We should be getting on," said Myrtle. "We'll be checking in on you later, Shay."

Shay thanked them profusely for the food and walked them out.

As Miles drove away, he said, "What did you make of all that?"

"I thought Shay's stilted, rather Victorian phrasing of her penniless days prior to Palmer smacked of something she overheard Palmer say more than once."

Miles nodded. "Right. The self-congratulatory Palmer."

"She seemed quite smug about her 'charity work,' as she called it. As far as my other impressions go, I think Cash wasn't the best of husbands. It sounds as if the two of them fought over money at least some of the time."

Miles said, "And now he's slated to get most of Palmer's estate."

"It's definitely the sort of thing that makes you think," said Myrtle. "Maybe Cash became tired of having to ask his wife's permission for big purchases."

Miles said, "What about his alibi, though?"

"I'd like to find out if it really *is* an alibi. Maybe Perkins will help me out. He could have come in on an earlier flight, gone home, seen his wife leaving the house very early, followed her at a distance, and then seen his opportunity."

"It all seems sort of cloak and dagger for a domestic crime. Wouldn't he just have found a way to murder Palmer at their home?"

"Not if he didn't want to be suspected. This way, he can at least tell the cops he was on his way back from a red-eye flight. I know they'll check with the airlines to confirm it, though."

Miles said, "What's on the agenda now? Are we heading back to your house to work on some puzzles?"

Myrtle frowned at him. "We don't have time for crosswords and sudoku, Miles. We have a case to solve."

"I have the feeling it won't be wrapped up today. We could take a short break." Miles's voice was hopeful.

"I don't think we've made enough progress to be able to take a break. All we know right now is that we don't like Cash."

Miles said, "I think we know more than that."

"We know we didn't like Palmer, either. That hardly helps."

Miles said, "It helps because we know there might have been plenty of suspects."

Myrtle tapped her fingers on her arm. "I know precisely what we need to do now. We need to talk with Bitsy."

Miles was quiet for a moment. "Do we? I'm not at all sure we need to speak with Puddin's cousin."

"I am. Puddin revealed that Bitsy said Palmer was having an affair."

Miles pulled into Myrtle's driveway. "That sounds like second or third-hand knowledge."

"It doesn't mean it's not true. We need to talk with Bitsy to find out."

Miles sighed. "You just got your house cleaned for book club. It doesn't need any cleaning."

Myrtle beamed at him. "An excellent observation, Miles. There's also the fact that I can't afford Bitsy's cleaning services. That's why you'll need to arrange to have Bitsy run by and clean your place."

"My house is perfectly clean."

"I wouldn't say that. It's very, very tidy, yes. Your books are arranged alphabetically by author in your bookcase. The pictures on your walls are all perfectly aligned. There isn't a sign of paper clutter anywhere. But I've noticed a fine layer of dust on your flat surfaces. And I believe your appliances could use a wiping down."

Miles looked horrified at the idea that he might have dust and objects that should be wiped down.

"Let's just call Bitsy and see what she can do." Myrtle pulled out her phone to look up Bitsy's website and call her.

"She'll be busy. You've always said she's completely booked out. Besides, I occasionally use Puddin for cleaning and she might be miffed."

Myrtle gave him a reproving look. "Don't balk, Miles. It's most unbecoming. And Puddin is constantly miffed at one thing or another." Myrtle tapped Bitsy's number into her phone and cleared her throat. "Bitsy? It's Myrtle Clover. How are you today? My friend Miles is in a jam today and wondered if you could come by and help him out with his house. No, I wouldn't say it needs much work, just some maintenance and a little deep cleaning, as well."

Miles glowered at her.

"Right now? Yes, he's completely free. Wonderful." Myrtle gave Bitsy Miles's address and hung up the phone with a satisfied smile.

Miles grumbled, "She's coming over right now, then?"

"She had a last-minute cancellation, so this works great. Oh, don't look so deeply unhappy, Miles. You'll be amazed how your place sparkles after she's done with it."

"It's sparkly enough as it is."

Myrtle wasn't listening, though. She was getting the key to her house out. "I'm going to dash inside to grab puzzles for us to work on while Bitsy's there."

Miles gloomily waited in the car while Myrtle retrieved the puzzles and a couple of her favorite pens. She also put some of Miles's favorite cookies in her purse in the hopes of sweetening his mood. It was most annoying when he got into one of his snits.

Several minutes later, they were settled at Miles's house. It was just in time, too, because Bitsy rang the bell shortly after. Myrtle looked admiringly at Bitsy as she came in. She wore a crisp pair of khaki pants and a pastel golf shirt with "Bitsy's Cleaning Services" embroidered on it. What was more, she was accompanied by a vacuum cleaner and a box of cleaning supplies. She gave them a cheerful smile. "Thanks for thinking of me today. Miles, do you mind showing me around the house a little and pointing out areas that might need special attention?"

Miles politely thanked her for coming by. Then he looked at Myrtle and said, "Actually, Myrtle might be the better one to show you all the places that require cleaning."

Although Miles perhaps meant to put Myrtle on the spot, she was delighted at the opportunity to speak with Bitsy. She abandoned her crossword puzzle and escorted Bitsy into Miles's kitchen. "Well, Miles is a fairly tidy person, but I believe his appliances need some wiping down."

Bitsy quickly walked through, evaluating the various kitchen appliances with a narrowed, expert gaze. "Got it."

"And his baseboards could use some work. Older people have trouble with baseboards."

Miles was now looking even more melancholy than he had previously.

Myrtle continued through Miles's small house, pointing out small things as she went. Then she said, "I'm glad you're here, Bitsy. We would have called Puddin, but—you know."

Bitsy did indeed know. She smiled and diplomatically said, "Sometimes it's hard to motivate Puddin."

"Yes." That was an understatement. It seemed to Myrtle that Bitsy had perhaps been gifted with all the initiative in that particular family.

"Although Puddin can be wonderful for entertaining me. She came by earlier and cooked for me."

This surprised Bitsy, who glanced up from the list she was making of Miles's "problem areas." Bitsy said, "Puddin did?"

"She did indeed. She cooked a marvelous chicken and dumplings for me to take over to Shay, Palmer's cousin. A bereavement dish, you know."

Bitsy, for all of her efficiency, dearly loved gossip. She gathered it lovingly, like someone with a cherished collection. "I think Puddin told me that you and Miles discovered Palmer."

Myrtle gave her a solemn nod. "I understand that you worked for Palmer and Cash?"

"Still do, at least as far as I know. They have a big house and they need help taking care of it all. Naturally, when I clean their house, I have to mark off the entire day on my calendar."

Myrtle said innocently in her best nosy-old-lady voice, "And I'm sure you know a lot of what transpired there behind closed doors, don't you? It would be difficult *not* to pick up on that sort of thing. After all, there you are working while life is unfolding all around you. I hear you believed Palmer might have been having an affair?"

Bitsy flushed slightly and there was a look that flashed in her eyes that boded ill for Puddin when she saw her again. "I suppose Puddin must have told you that," she said with a sigh.

"She did indeed."

Bitsy said slowly, "Palmer was seeing someone. I kind of felt sorry for her, though."

"Sorry? For Palmer?" This was a surprise to Myrtle. Palmer, for all her "charity work" wasn't the most sympathetic of characters.

"Mm-hm. Because she was just retaliating because she knew her husband was playing around on her." Bitsy raised her eyebrows.

"Gracious," said Myrtle, playing up the old-lady angle even more. "Was he?"

"Not just was, *is*. I can even tell you who he's having the affair with." She pursed her lips. "I don't want you to think I'm a horrible person for gossiping."

"Of course I don't. It's information sharing, isn't it, Bitsy? You're just trying to process what you know. And my lips are sealed, of course."

Bitsy looked a little concerned. "You won't tell Red?"

Myrtle snorted. "I certainly won't. He has to find out things out on his own." Besides, Myrtle was determined to follow her own leads and solve the case before he did. She fingered her medic alert necklace.

Satisfied, Bitsy said, "Well, Cash has been seeing my roommate. You know, with housing so expensive and everything, I save money by sharing a place with Mariah."

"Mariah," said Myrtle thoughtfully. "I know a Mariah. And it's not the most common of names, is it?"

"You might know her from the diner. She works there."

"The very Mariah I was thinking of," said Myrtle, nodding. "So, the two of them are an item?"

Bitsy made a face. "I'm afraid so. I don't think much of Cash and I'm hoping the two of them will break up. He's no good for her. The problem is that Mariah is way too invested in him, you know?"

"She's fallen for him."

"In a big way. And I can tell that Cash just doesn't feel the same way. He's totally using her. Plus, he always acts . . . remote. You know? It always feels to me like he thinks he's just too good for us."

Myrtle said wryly, "If it makes you feel better, he acts like that around everybody. I've heard the same thing said about his behavior with Palmer. And, from what I've experienced of Cash, he was the same around me."

Bitsy put her hands on her hips. "Well, it doesn't come across well. I've got my fingers crossed that the two of them will break up soon. It makes me sad that a break-up is going to hurt Mariah, though. She has all these dreams that Cash will want to marry her now that he's a widower."

Myrtle considered this. It certainly appeared that Mariah had a motive for murdering Palmer. "That does sound like a mess. Do you know who Palmer was seeing? For her retaliatory affair?"

Bitsy nodded. "Yes ma'am. And that's the part that makes me *not* feel sorry for Palmer. She could have had an affair with anybody she wanted to, you know?"

"Indeed. Palmer was a very attractive and intelligent woman."

"Right. And she was seeing Hiram Hudson." Bitsy waited for a reaction.

Myrtle raised both her eyebrows. "Hiram? But he's her best friend's husband."

Bitsy just nodded again.

"And Whitley is about to have a baby." Myrtle was incensed on Whitley's behalf.

"Palmer was something else, wasn't she?"

Myrtle just pressed her lips together.

Bitsy glanced at her watch and said gently, "I've loved talking with you, Miss M. If I'm going to stay on schedule and get

Mr. Bradford's house sparkling, though, I'm going to have to get to work."

"Of course, my dear. Hop to it. But I did so enjoy our talk."

Bitsy gave her a smile and set to with the dusting.

Myrtle returned to Miles who was looking rather miserable in the living room. "What on earth's the problem? Your house will be shining."

"I'm not fond of being around when people are working in my house. It makes me feel like I'm overseeing their progress."

Myrtle sighed. "The funniest things make you uncomfortable, Miles. I watch Puddin's every move because, if I don't, she'll be watching game shows and eating potato chips from my pantry. If it makes you feel better, let's sit in your backyard. That way, you'll be available if Bitsy has any questions for you."

Myrtle grabbed their puzzles and Miles poured them a couple of glasses of water. Miles's backyard was immaculate because he hired an excellent landscaping service to take care of it. The bushes were trimmed into geometrical shapes which Myrtle couldn't help but think wasn't good for the shrubs. They did look very Miles-like, however. There were some wrought-iron chairs around a table. The chairs didn't look particularly comfortable. But then Miles reached into a storage bench and pulled out some navy cushions which he proceeded to place on the chairs.

Myrtle laid out their puzzles, pens, and pencils. But Miles was more interested in what had transpired between Myrtle and Bitsy.

"Considering your elaborate set-up to collect information from Bitsy, I'd like to know how you fared," said Miles.

"Extremely well. Bitsy is a veritable fount of information. From our short conversation, I was able to learn that not only was Palmer having an affair with her best friend's husband, but that Cash is currently having an affair with Mariah from the diner."

Miles's eyes widened behind his glasses.

"That's right. I don't even know where to start dissecting all of that. It definitely doesn't make me feel very sympathetic toward Palmer, although Bitsy said that her affair was spurred by the fact that she realized Cash was having one."

"How does Bitsy know all this?" asked Miles. "And is it true?"

"Oh, I think it's definitely true. Bitsy has always had her finger on the pulse of the town. While she's working in people's houses, she's learning a lot about them and the lives they're living."

Miles looked very uncomfortable. "That's not exactly a comforting thought."

"The only thing Bitsy is going to find out about you, Miles, is that you have stomach issues and a propensity toward hypochondria. That's hardly the sort of thing that will have the town of Bradley buzzing."

Miles looked as if he couldn't decide whether it was better to be boring or not.

Myrtle said thoughtfully, "Do you remember when Mariah came into the diner after we found Palmer?"

Miles nodded. "I'd thought at the time she looked startled to see the policemen there."

"Exactly. But now I'm thinking she wasn't startled at the police presence but at *Cash's* presence. That's when Cash was in the diner sitting with us while Red and Perkins asked him questions."

"Makes sense," said Miles.

Myrtle continued thoughtfully, "So. Hiram Hudson."

"Hmm?"

"Hiram. He's Whitley's husband. The one Palmer is having the affair with."

Miles said delicately, "And Whitley is expecting, I believe."

"Most certainly. She rather looked as if she were expecting triplets. I think we should pay a visit to Hiram."

"How do you plan on managing that?" asked Miles. "I don't even know who he is."

"That's because you don't golf, Miles. Perhaps that's something we should think about changing."

Miles immediately shook his head. "No way, Myrtle. I have next to no interest in golf."

"You watch the Masters Tournament every year!"

"Only because it's very lulling. If I've had a difficult day, watching golf can be soothing. All those muted voices of the commentators on the television. I have *no* desire to take up the sport." He sounded particularly resolute.

"All right, then. I suppose *I* could take up golf."

Miles shook his head again. "Red won't like that. You'll be teetering around without your cane, contorting your body into odd positions to strike the ball. It sounds like the perfect storm for a fall."

"I have my medic alert necklace," said Myrtle with a sniff.

"You know perfectly well that it doesn't work outside your house. Besides, there's one other aspect of golfing you haven't considered."

"What's that?" asked Myrtle, sounding aggravated.

"The cost. It's hideously expensive to golf. There are green fees. There are country club fees. There are golf pro fees. Then there's the equipment. There's a reason why half the golfers out there are doctors."

Myrtle sighed. "You're right—I forgot about that. There's no way my dinky little budget could include golfing of any kind."

"I take it Hiram works at the country club in some capacity?"

Myrtle nodded. "He's the golf pro there." She brightened. "We could *pretend* we were interested in golfing."

Miles stubbornly shook his head.

Myrtle thought some more. "I know. I could say I wanted to get more information about *Red* taking up golfing. That perhaps I was thinking about springing for lessons for him. That at least will give us the opportunity to talk with him." She glanced at her watch. "The way Bitsy moves, she'll be done here in no time. Then you and I will take a field trip to the country club."

Miles couldn't look less pleased.

# Chapter Ten

After Myrtle had completed two crossword puzzles and Miles two sudokus, Bitsy popped her head out the door.

"All done," she said with a smile. "Mr. Bradford, would you like to take a look and make sure I didn't miss any spots?"

Miles got up and Myrtle collected their puzzles and followed. Miles blinked as he looked around his glimmering, spotless house.

"It looks perfect," he said slowly.

Bitsy looked pleased. "Glad you think I did a good job."

A few minutes later, Miles had paid Bitsy for the cleaning and saw her out.

Myrtle said smugly, "I thought you'd be pleased with Bitsy's work."

"The house looked fine to begin with, but when it's *that* clean, you realize how messy it actually was at the beginning."

Miles then plopped down on his sofa. "I have a confession to make."

"That sounds ominous."

"I'm very tired. I watched nature shows in the middle of the night, discovered a dead body at our favorite eating place, and then inflicted myself on the victim's cousin. What's more, I had my house cleaned from top to bottom by someone who is basically a stranger to me. I believe I'm done for the day, Myrtle. No country club for me."

"I suppose I could borrow your car," said Myrtle thoughtfully. Then she frowned. "No, I think I'd rather have you with me when I speak with Hiram. It will lend more credibility to our visit."

"I'm not sure how, considering I don't golf."

"No, but you know the golfing lingo. It won't do for me to interview Hiram on my own. I'll go bright and early tomorrow morning with you."

Miles yawned and nodded. "Mornings would likely be better, anyway. Most people are working and it likely won't be busy over there as it would be in the late afternoon."

"For heaven's sake, get some rest. I'll need you to be bright-eyed and bushy-tailed when we speak with Hiram tomorrow."

Miles, fortunately, was able to sleep that night and was over at Myrtle's before eight. They had coffee together, worked a puzzle, then set off to see Hiram.

The country club was a venerable institution in Bradley and its appearance showed it. The building had a weathered appearance about it. There was an ancient swimming pool that desperately needed updating. The landscaping was spotty. The golf course, however, was fairly decently maintained and quite popular among the golfing crowd. Myrtle could see several golf carts puttering around as they approached.

"I suppose we should go to the golf shop," said Myrtle with a frown. "Hiram should be there unless he's giving lessons, I suppose."

The golf shop was also rather dated looking. It had wood paneling that made the shop quite dim, despite the fluorescent lighting. The apparel looked rather sparse. Myrtle immediately spotted Hiram, a preppy-looking man of about 40 years with blonde hair, blue eyes, and a weak mouth. He glanced up, looking surprised as Myrtle approached. He quickly covered up his surprise with a warm smile.

"Miss Myrtle," he said. "What a pleasure to see you here today."

"The pleasure is all mine, Hiram. Miles, Hiram was one of my favorite pupils back in the day. I'll never forget that he gave me a wheeled desk chair when he graduated from high school."

Hiram's jovial tone sounded a bit practiced—the sort of voice a golf pro might often need to employ. "Well, you wrote me some excellent recommendation letters for school. And I loved every minute of my college years."

"As I recall, you were accepted to every school you applied to."

Hiram nodded. "An excellent memory as always, Miss Myrtle."

She beamed at him. "And now perhaps I should get to the purpose of my little visit. I've been thinking about giving Red a gift. I've been mulling on it for a while and I believe the best type of present I can give him is an *experience*. An experience doesn't take up any space and Red and Elaine have wall-to-wall toys in their house because of little Jack."

Hiram chuckled. "I bet that's the case. Whitley and I are going to find out soon enough, I suppose."

"Yes, Miles and I saw Whitley at book club. She's looking marvelous. When is she due?"

Hiram said, "In about another month. We're just glad everything is going well so far and that Whitley has been feeling so good."

"That certainly is a blessing not to have to deal with morning sickness or any of that nonsense."

Hiram said, "So, I'm guessing golf is the experience you're considering gifting Red? That's very nice. Is it his birthday?"

Myrtle shook her head. "No special occasion. I just wanted to . . . celebrate him, I suppose. And he did give me this lovely necklace."

She gestured to the medic alert button on the lanyard and Hiram quickly said, "That's lovely, indeed. And very thoughtful of Red."

Miles smiled, thinking of the necklace and Red's debatable thoughtfulness.

"Yes. I was thinking that golf lessons might be a good gift for him. Could you let me know about how much those would run me?"

Hiram said, "Absolutely. If you're thinking about a thirty-minute lesson, it will be thirty dollars."

"Mercy!"

Hiram gave his retired teacher a rueful look. "Expensive, aren't they?"

"I'll say. I'll have to contemplate that some more."

Miles cleared his throat. "It's a very expensive hobby," he said meaningfully to Myrtle. He wanted to make sure Myrtle wasn't carried away and actually purchased the lessons.

Hiram said apologetically, "Miles is right. The golf equipment isn't particularly cheap, either. He'll need clubs and other things."

"Oh, I figured I could just pick those things up used." Myrtle waved her hand airily. "The point is that he's talked about golfing for years and has never done anything about it."

Miles gave her a doubtful look. He'd never heard Red's name in conjunction with golf before.

"Life is short. That's why I thought about the lessons. You never know when your time may be up. Like poor Palmer."

Hiram's face grew serious. "Yes."

Myrtle said sternly, "Now Hiram, there's something I must mention to you. I do hate to bring up something so personal, but it simply must be done. Since I care about you, as your former teacher, I think you need to know what's being said so you can put the rumors to rest."

Hiram swallowed. He looked as if he had an idea what the rumors might be about.

"I've heard, through the Bradley rumor mill, that you and Palmer were . . . seeing each other."

A red flush rose from Hiram's collared shirt and up his face. He spluttered, "I don't know how anyone would know about that."

Miles gave a commiserating sigh. "Small towns. I'm only just now getting used to it."

Myrtle said, "The point is, Hiram, if *I* know, then it's only a matter of time until *Red* knows. And then? Well, Red might put two-and-two together and come up with an incorrect version of events."

Hiram sank down into a nearby chair and Myrtle and Miles followed suit.

In a shaky voice, Hiram said, "You've got to believe me, Miss Myrtle. I had nothing to do with Palmer's death. I was on the golf course early to check the ground conditions for the golfers and arrange for early tee times."

Myrtle nodded in an understanding way. "I guess, though, from Red's point of view, there wouldn't have been anyone around to verify that."

Beads of sweat started appearing on his handsome face. He took a deep breath in an apparent attempt to calm down, but he still managed to look extremely flustered.

"I'll admit Palmer and I had . . . a relationship. It was not my finest moment, nor was it Palmer's. We'd just recently decided, mutually, that we weren't going to continue seeing each other."

"You split up," said Myrtle.

He nodded. "Completely amicably."

"It wasn't a 'love match,' then," said Myrtle delicately.

Hiram said, "Not at all. Palmer was just going through a rough patch in her marriage to Cash, that's all. And I'm not sure what I was doing." He sounded irritated with himself.

"How bad of a bad patch was it?"

Hiram rubbed his face. "They weren't getting along well at all. I'm not sure they ever have. But it was a lot worse lately. The reason I can say that is because they were sniping at each other in front of friends instead of just behind closed doors. To be honest, I had the feeling both of them were going to be heading to the divorce courts soon. Then *this* happened."

"I understand there might have been some disagreements over money."

Hiram gave a humorless laugh. "The rumor mill in Bradley is definitely still working. I guess some of their problems were money-related, sure. The issue was that Palmer came in with gobs of her own money and Cash felt like he wasn't contributing that much."

Miles cleared his throat. "You're friends with Cash, then?"

Hiram looked even more miserable. "Yeah. I know that sounds awful. We became friends pretty much as soon as they moved to town. Cash was interested in finding a group to play golf with. He and I started hanging out after that."

"But Cash has a good job, doesn't he?" asked Myrtle with a frown.

"He seems to. He's always flying here and there for it. I think he's a manager of some kind in the company he works for. He definitely pulls in a lot more money than I do," said Hiram with that short, flat laugh again. He paused for a moment and then said in a worried voice, "You really think Red is going to find out? About Palmer and me, I mean?"

Myrtle sighed. "I have to imagine he will, Hiram. Red gets on my last nerve, but he's a pretty smart man. At least your relationship with Palmer was over."

Hiram brightened. "That's got to count for something, doesn't it? I'd started thinking about Whitley and the baby, you know. I'm going to be a father—which somehow kind of sneaked up on me. When you first find out, it feels like nine months is going to take forever. But it totally flies. I started realizing that I needed to make my relationship with Whitley work for both of our sakes and for the sake of the baby."

Miles nodded approvingly. "Very wise of you."

Hiram continued, "Marriages have good days and bad days. Before, the bad days made me just want to escape. But now I know I need to stick around for both the good and the bad. That I need to be fully present."

Myrtle said, "I do think that's a very good approach, Hiram, and I'm sure you'll find everything improves in your marriage."

He looked pleased. "I hope so." His face clouded again. "I guess now I just have to worry that I might get dragged into the investigation of Palmer's death."

"Did Whitley know about your indiscretion?"

Hiram paled at the thought. "Absolutely not. And I plan to keep it that way. I've been wanting this baby for a long time and now I'm ready to be a good family man. I can't have word like that leaking out."

Myrtle said, "Do you have any idea why Palmer might have been at the diner so early in the morning? It wasn't even open yet."

"Wasn't it?" asked Hiram. "I thought I'd heard that you and Miles were there and found Palmer. Which must have been devastating."

"It was," said Myrtle, a bit unconvincingly. "But Miles and I were mistaken about the diner's hours. Only the staff was there at the time."

Hiram said, "I see. Well, it must have had to do with her plans to buy the diner."

"Did she talk about that with you?"

Hiram nodded. "All the time. I thought she was pretty obsessed with the idea. She kept showing me plans she had for the place."

"What did you think about them?"

Hiram shrugged. "The plans were fine, I guess. She was basically going to gut the place, get rid of the staff, and completely change everything about the restaurant. It was going to be a French bistro or something. The food wasn't going to be the same at all. I mean, Palmer always seemed to do a great job at everything she set out to do. I knew it would end up looking fantastic and she'd end up with a good cook. The problem was that I didn't think anybody in Bradley would be happy about losing Bo's Diner."

Myrtle said, "I think you pegged it, Hiram. My thoughts, exactly. In fact, I don't think Bo himself was happy with Palmer's ideas. My understanding was that she'd tried to convince him to sell the place to her before and was rejected."

Hiram snorted. "Yeah, that's what happened. Palmer wasn't used to any kind of rejection—it made her flip out. So then she doubled down and tried to persuade him to sell the diner to her. She talked about it constantly. Palmer even had me pretend to be Bo and she gave her whole presentation as practice."

Miles said slowly, "I don't understand why she'd want to present her sales pitch to Bo so early in the morning. The whole staff was hustling trying to get the diner ready for the breakfast crowd."

He said wryly, "Palmer probably thought it was effective to totally blindside Bo to get her way. Palmer would be organized, ultra-professional, and persuasive. She'd be angry, too, since she was used to getting her way. Palmer would hope to surprise Bo and catch him off-guard."

"She sounds like a force to be reckoned with," said Miles.

Hiram nodded.

Myrtle said, "Hiram, it sounds as if you might have understood what was going on in Palmer's life at the time. Was there anyone she talked about who had some sort of grievance against her? Did she run into trouble with anyone?"

Hiram considered this. Then he said, "I don't know if Palmer even really registered that. I mean, she made people unhappy with her all the time. She was like a steamroller—used to powering through and getting her way with everything. She never mentioned anybody unhappy enough with her to do her in, that's for sure."

"So no ideas who might be behind her death?" Myrtle gave him a stern look as if she'd expected her former pupil to do better.

Hiram saw the look and immediately tried to come up with a better answer. "Well, I guess her husband is the most-likely suspect. After all, the spouse is usually the one who's responsible. Cash and I have been friendly with each other, though, and I can't picture him murdering anyone. He wouldn't want to get his hands dirty. Besides Cash, I think Palmer's cousin could potentially be a suspect, too."

"Shay?" asked Myrtle.

He nodded. "Palmer didn't treat her well."

Myrtle raised her eyebrows. "Shay seemed to think she had."

Hiram said, "Palmer treated her well in terms of giving her a place to stay and food and things like that. But Palmer complained about Shay all the time. She was either complaining about her or bragging that she had basically scooped Shay off the streets and turned her life around."

Miles made a face. "That would get old fast."

"Are we sure Shay would harm the person who provided her with a home, though?" Myrtle's voice was doubtful.

Hiram said, "Maybe she got so fed-up with Palmer that she just struck out at her."

Myrtle said, "But that would be an impulsive crime. Whoever killed Palmer would have followed her out to the diner before dawn."

Hiram shrugged. "Maybe she planned on talking to her privately and followed her car out? Then she could have lost her temper."

Miles could see that Hiram was rapidly losing interest in their visit. "Myrtle, shouldn't we be heading out?"

"Hmm?" Myrtle, still thinking things over, sounded a little vague.

"Shouldn't we leave? We have that thing we need to get to." He gave Myrtle a meaningful look.

"Oh. I suppose we should. It was very good to see you, Hiram. I'll be in touch about the lessons."

"Good to see you, too, Miss Myrtle."

# Chapter Eleven

As they walked to the car, Myrtle said, "You couldn't have come up with a genuine excuse? 'We have that thing we need to get to?'"

"I thought you'd catch on that Hiram was ready for us to go."

Myrtle shook her head. "No, I was thinking about the case."

They climbed into Miles's black sedan. Miles said, "What conclusions did you come up with during your mulling?"

"Nothing too concrete. It does seem like Shay might have gotten irritated with Palmer for treating her like a charity case. That wouldn't be fun for anyone."

Miles drove away from the country club. "Plus there was that thing about the animals."

"For heaven's sake, Miles! You're not being very coherent today. What thing about the animals are you referring to?"

Miles stopped at a stop sign and turned to look at Myrtle. "You remember. It was when we were visiting Shay and she was talking about how she worked at the animal shelter."

"Ah. Yes. We asked if she had a bunch of rescues at her cottage and she indicated that Cash didn't want any pets there. Hmm. You're right—for someone like Shay, that would be very aggravating. But was it aggravating enough for Shay to hop in her car, follow Palmer under cloak of darkness, and murder her benefactor? It seems unlikely."

"The whole thing seems unlikely," said Miles. "Palmer was annoying. She was a do-gooder. She got on everyone's nerves.

But would you kill someone because she got on your nerves? I think it has more to do with the Bo's Diner sale. Maybe somebody on the staff didn't want to lose their job. Or maybe Bo got tired of Palmer's pushiness and killed her on the spur of the moment."

Myrtle considered this. "But that would mean Bo was skulking out in the parking lot."

"Maybe Palmer and Bo drove up to the diner at the same time. That truck of Palmer's is very recognizable. He might have walked over to see what she was there for. Then he struck her in a rage over the fact that she wouldn't let the sale of the diner go."

Myrtle tilted her head to one side. "But Bo? I've known him since he was in diapers. He's the most laid-back person in that whole family. Now Bo's grandfather, God bless his soul? He'd have murdered somebody in a skinny second just for looking at him the wrong way. I simply can't picture Bo having done it. But I do hear what you're saying—we've been talking about how Palmer's death seems premeditated because she was followed to the diner very early in the morning. But Bo would have already been there so it *could* have been spontaneous."

Miles pulled up to Myrtle's house and she blinked at it as if surprised to find herself there. "I didn't want to come back home. We need to keep investigating."

"Shouldn't we take a break? Maybe have some iced tea and watch the tape of *Tomorrow's Promise*?"

Myrtle frowned at him. "You certainly are caught up in that storyline, Miles. You're determined to find out if Marissa can escape from the cave."

"It's very suspenseful." Miles's face was slightly flushed.

"I do believe you have a crush on Marissa. I'm sure she'll find her way out of that cave. After all, I haven't read anything in *Soap Opera Weekly* about the actress's contract not being renewed. And yes, hydrating and relaxing is good. I just was planning on doing that *after* we asked a few more questions."

"Who are you wanting to talk to next?" Miles looked a bit apprehensive.

"Whitley Hudson."

Miles groaned. "I was afraid you were going to say that. Should we really go over and harass a woman who's expecting? I don't want to pay the consequences for that. What if the stress induces her into labor or something?"

"For heaven's sake, Miles. It's not as if we'll give her the third degree. It will be very genteel conversation with a few well-crafted questions mixed in."

Miles still looked queasy at the idea of someone spontaneously bursting into labor around him. "I'd rather not."

Myrtle said, "Think about it. She's just lost her very best friend in Bradley. She's very, very pregnant, if you can qualify something like pregnancy. Her hormones are all over the place."

Miles looked even more displeased at the mention of hormones.

Myrtle said, "Plus, she's a brand-new member of our book club. The very least we can do is to head over there with a little food and our sympathy."

Miles shook his head vehemently. "No way. Not food. She might be on a special diet."

"It's a pregnancy, not a disease."

Miles didn't appear to be willing to budge on this point, however. "Nope. No food."

Myrtle heaved a long-suffering sigh. "I don't know what's gotten into you. I suppose we could bring her something else. Perhaps something for the baby."

Miles looked relieved. "Yes. Something for the baby would be perfect."

"Is it a boy or a girl?" Myrtle frowned. "I can't remember if Whitley said or not. I suppose it doesn't really matter. We can always get something like a small stuffed animal or something. Jack had one that played nursery tunes when you wound it up. We could find something like that. Let's head to the department store."

Thirty minutes later, and a gift-wrapped musical lamb in tow, Myrtle and Miles headed for Whitley Hudson's house.

As they walked up the walkway to the modest ranch-style house, Miles said grimly, "Now remember—we're not going to upset Whitley."

"I wouldn't dream of it. Upset people often cry and that's the last thing in the world I want."

They rang the doorbell, and soon Whitley answered. She looked like a shadow of her former self.

"Oh, Miss Myrtle. And Mr. Bradford. Can I help you with something?"

Myrtle briskly said, "We don't need a thing from you, dear. We just wanted to bring a little something on behalf of book club to say we were so very sorry about Palmer and that we are thinking of you."

With that, Whitley heartily burst into tears. Myrtle winced and Miles gave Myrtle a reproving look. Myrtle shrugged.

"Here, let's go inside and have a seat," said Myrtle, hustling Whitley into the house.

"I'll fix you a glass of water," said Miles, looking relieved at having a mission that would take him away, at least momentarily, from the sobbing Whitley.

Whitley sank into a rather threadbare armchair. Fortunately, there was a box of tissues right next to her. From all appearances, the tissues had been frequently used. There were used ones in a nearly-full wastebasket next to her chair.

Miles, who'd stalled just about as long as he possibly could on his very simple errand, returned with the glass of ice water.

Myrtle was saying in a soothing voice, "There now, Whitley, you're just fine. Take some deep breaths. Things will look better before long."

Whitley wiped her eyes and then said, "Thanks so much. I'm so sorry about this. I just can't believe Palmer is gone." She took a shuddering breath and then a sip from the glass of water.

Myrtle and Miles waited for a minute while Whitley calmed herself down. Then she gave them a weak smile. "Again, I'm sorry. Everything seems to be triggering me to start crying right now."

Myrtle nodded quickly, wanting to move forward before Whitley dissolved into tears again. "Of course it is. That's only natural, isn't it? Why don't you open your gift?"

She gave that weak smile again and unwrapped the present. When Whitley saw the musical lamb she said, "Oh, how sweet!"

"Wind it up," said Myrtle.

Whitley did, and *Twinkle, Twinkle Little Star* played. Whitley burst into tears again.

Miles gave Myrtle an anxious look.

"There, there," said Myrtle briskly. "You'll be all right, Whitley. You've just had something very disturbing happen, after all." Myrtle suspected Whitley was also afflicted by some sort of horrid hormonal attack.

Whitley sniffled and appeared to pull herself together, much to Myrtle's relief. "Yes," said Whitley in a shaky voice. "Gosh, I'm so sorry, y'all. You must think I'm such a disaster. And I'm in your book club and everything." She sighed. "I'm not much of a reader, I'm afraid. You've been so sweet to give me a lamb, but I have the feeling I'm going to have to drop out of your club. Palmer was the one who was the reader. And now I'm about to have a baby. It just isn't the best time."

"Why don't you let a little time pass and see how you feel? Things might look a bit more manageable later on. You've just lost your friend, after all."

Whitley nodded. "And I've been feeling very lonely today. Hiram had to go to work, of course."

"Yes, we saw him today, actually."

"Did you?" Whitley's eyes widened with surprise. "At the golf course?"

Apparently, Whitley couldn't quite picture the octogenarian Myrtle juggling her cane and a golf club.

"I was interested in the possibility of giving Red some golf lessons as a gift. I don't think I quite realized how expensive they are, though."

"Oh, they're horribly expensive," agreed Whitley.

Myrtle was curious whether Whitley knew anything at all of the affair. It certainly seemed she didn't since she was so very upset over Palmer's untimely demise. Surely, if she'd realized her best friend had betrayed her like that, she wouldn't have been quite so devastated. Still, Myrtle thought she might tiptoe around the issue.

"I'm sure Hiram was also a friend of Palmer's?" asked Myrtle innocently.

Miles gave Myrtle a stern look. He clearly didn't want any further display of emotion from Whitley, no matter what form it might take.

Whitley blinked at her. "Hiram? I suppose he was a friend of sorts. He hung out more with Cash of course. But the four of us would have dinner at Palmer's house all the time." Her eyes clouded. "I think I'm still in shock over it all. I told Hiram I was fine so that he would go on to work today. We need the income with a baby on the way. But I'm really not fine. I just keep thinking that I was fast asleep when my best friend was being attacked. What kind of a friend is that?"

"A friend who's about to have a baby and needs to get her rest," said Myrtle pragmatically. "It was also very early in the morning. I suppose Hiram was asleep, too?"

Whitley nodded. "We were sound asleep. And then a friend called me later in the morning to tell me how sorry she was to hear about Palmer. I didn't even know!"

Miles raised his eyebrows at Myrtle, wanting to see if she could calm Whitley down a little. She gave Miles an aggravated look but said, "Were you and Palmer friends as soon as she and Cash moved to town?"

"We sure were. The two of us were like peas in a pod. We had all the same interests—shopping, clothes, clubs. We always had so much fun together. I just have such a hard time wrapping my head around the fact that somebody hated her enough to kill her."

Myrtle said, "No ideas, dear? No mean looks from anyone? No one saying anything snide to Palmer?"

Whitley considered this. "Well, there was this woman who was stalking Palmer."

"*Stalking* her?"

"Sort of. She was bothering her, anyway. She kept coming over to Palmer's house and ringing her doorbell or coming up to Palmer when she was in the grocery store. Stuff like that. All I know is that Palmer found her seriously annoying and told her off."

Myrtle wondered if this was Nancy Young—the woman who couldn't pay back the loan Palmer had given her. "Could you describe the woman? Maybe she could somehow be involved."

Whitley flushed. "Oh, I hate the idea of getting someone into trouble, especially if they didn't do anything."

"No one can get into trouble if there's no evidence against them," said Myrtle smoothly. It wasn't exactly the truth, but it seemed to assuage Whitley's fears.

"I see. Well, she was middle-aged, I guess. I could tell she chewed her fingernails because they looked awful. She had streaks of gray in her hair and a sort of a slouch to her shoulders."

It was a perfect description of Nancy Young.

"That's very helpful, my dear. It's good to get an idea of who might be responsible for Palmer's death. That way, justice can finally be done."

Whitley straightened a little in her chair. "That's true. And it makes me feel better. I'd like to help find who did this, for Palmer's sake. I just feel so *useless*. Maybe this is a clue that can help crack the case."

Myrtle doubted it, considering the fact Red was already aware of Nancy Young because of his conversation with Cash. But she smiled sweetly at Whitley just the same.

"We should leave you now," said Myrtle. "Maybe you can put your feet up for a bit and get some rest."

Whitley tried struggling to her feet but Miles quickly said, "We're able to see ourselves out."

And they left as Whitley called out her thanks for the lamb and her goodbyes.

Miles started up the car. "Where will we continue our reign of terror next?"

"Reign of terror?"

"It just seems like wherever we go, people start crying," said Miles morosely.

"That's only because they've recently suffered the death of someone close to them. It has nothing whatsoever to do with us."

Miles just sighed.

"And, to answer your question, we'll head to the Piggly Wiggly."

Miles looked concerned at the mention of the grocery store. "Why?"

"How suspicious you sound, Miles! I only want to go there because the milk is on sale this week. The price of milk is completely absurd. Sometimes I think I'd do better if I purchased a cow."

"I'm sure Red would love the addition of livestock to your yard."

"It could mill around in harmony with the gnomes," said Myrtle thoughtfully. "I wonder how much hay costs?"

"I thought they ate grass."

"Well, considering how difficult it can be to get Dusty over to mow the lawn, there should be plenty of that."

Miles pulled up to the grocery store. "Should I wait in the car?" he asked hopefully. "If you're only getting milk."

"I'm only getting milk. Just stay put and I'll be right back."

Myrtle hurried into the grocery store, cane thumping as she went. The way the grocery store was designed, the most important things were in the back of the store along the walls. This ensured Myrtle had to cut through one of her favorite aisles to get to the milk that was on sale. Which was how she became burdened with not only her cane, but crackers that were buy-two-get-three free.

Sadly, the crackers fell to the floor directly in front of the meat section.

Myrtle shot them a vicious look.

Suddenly, a woman appeared and, stooping, picked up the boxes from the floor. "Miss Myrtle?" she asked. "Are you okay?"

# Chapter Twelve

Myrtle recognized Nancy Young—the woman who was supposedly indebted to Palmer and couldn't pay her back. She immediately put on her doddering old lady act. "Goodness, thank you, Nancy. I don't know what I'd have done if you hadn't shown up. Left the crackers on the floor, I suppose."

Nancy was pushing a large and almost empty shopping cart. In the child seat, she had a large binder which had plastic envelopes full of coupons. Next to it was the weekly ad for the grocery store. On top of the ad was a calculator.

Nancy said, "How about if I give you a hand? You don't have a cart?"

Myrtle shook her head and said feebly, "I was just coming in for the milk. But I cut through the cracker aisle and my favorite brand was on sale. I guess I couldn't juggle everything."

"Let's put them in my cart and I'll walk with you to get the milk and to the checkout counter."

Myrtle beamed at her. "Wonderful. But let's replace these boxes of crackers first. I have the feeling I've smashed them to smithereens."

This was apparently contrary to Nancy's "if you break it, you buy it" philosophy. She hesitated and then hurried over to put the crackers in a neat stack on the floor in front of the display so that no one would purchase them. Then she retrieved some fresh boxes, carefully shaking them to ensure there was no sound of crumbs rattling around and placed them in the cart.

"There now," said Nancy. "Let's get the milk."

Myrtle moved very slowly in order to maximize the time she spent with Nancy. Nancy, accordingly, moved very slowly, too.

"I do admire your set-up here, Nancy. You have quite the approach to saving money." Myrtle waved her hand to indicate the coupons, ad, and calculator.

Nancy's face brightened at the compliment. "Thanks, Miss Myrtle. It's time-consuming, of course, but I save so much money. I also work here at the store, so I get an employee discount on some items. Today is my day off, though. Do you clip coupons?"

"Oh no, dear. I wouldn't have the patience. I just shop the ads. That's why I was in here for the milk. But I do think you're being very smart with your approach. Some people, of course, don't have to worry about such things. Palmer Hudson, bless her soul, didn't."

At this, Nancy flushed and accidentally knocked her coupon binder to the ground. She quickly stooped to pick it up, looking even more flustered.

"I'm sorry, Nancy," said Myrtle looking innocent. "Were you friends of Palmer's? I shouldn't have brought her up." Miles's comment about their reign of terror popped, unbidden, into her mind.

Nancy said, "Did you know her, Miss Myrtle? I'm surprised your paths crossed."

Myrtle noticed that Nancy hadn't answered the question. She said, "Oh, you know—book club, garden club. Palmer was something of a joiner, I suppose. I think she was a member of just about every organization in Bradley. I can only handle my two clubs and even they drive me batty. Did you know her from a club, too? Maybe the historical society? Or Friends of the Library?"

Nancy shook her head as they continued creeping toward the milk at a snail's pace. "No, I knew Palmer in more of a business sense, I guess. What happened to her was terrible, though. I was asleep when it happened, of course, and then came straight to the store. One of my customers told me about it later that morning."

Myrtle nodded. "I'm sure you must hear all the local gossip almost immediately. How is the job here?"

"They treat me pretty well. But all I have time for is sleeping and working. I pick up lots of shifts, but I don't mind. I need the money, and I was so relieved to get the job. I was trying to find work for a while and really couldn't. I wanted to work at the department store first, but they didn't have any openings at all. So the grocery store it was."

"I suppose you probably knew Palmer from the store, too," prompted Myrtle.

"I did. She knew I was struggling with money and tried to help me. Actually, she was the one who got me this job. Palmer knew the manager here." Then Nancy, to Myrtle's alarm, burst into tears. "She was the whole reason I got this grocery job."

"There, there," said Myrtle briskly, reaching into her voluminous handbag. "Here, have a tissue." Then, upon seeing the number of tears streaking down Nancy's cheeks, amended it to: "Just take the whole tissue packet."

Myrtle realized she might soon have to come back from the store to purchase more travel-sized tissues.

Once Nancy had calmed down enough to talk, she gave Myrtle a grateful look. "Thanks, Miss Myrtle."

"Of course. Dealing with death is hard, isn't it?"

Nancy nodded, sniffling into a tissue.

"I just can't imagine who might have done this to poor Palmer. I know you speak to a lot of folks here at the store. Have you heard anyone say anything against her?"

Nancy paused as if considering how best to answer the question. "I don't think Palmer was really popular, Miss Myrtle. You know how newcomers to town are treated."

Myrtle did indeed. A small town could be very insular. But Palmer brought a lot of her problems on herself.

"Was there anyone in particular who stands out as not caring much for Palmer?" asked Myrtle delicately.

Nancy started crying again, which set Myrtle's teeth on edge. Just then, she spotted Miles striding toward them. He stopped short when he saw Nancy sobbing. Rolling his eyes at Myrtle, he headed back for the door.

"I'm sorry," said Nancy. "I just don't know if I can throw somebody under the bus like that. It's such a sad situation."

"Oh, it's just me. I was simply curious." Myrtle crossed her fingers at the fib.

Nancy took a hiccupping breath. "It's just—well, it's Whitley."

Myrtle raised her eyebrows. "Whitley Hudson? Palmer's best friend?"

"That's right. That's what makes it so sad."

Myrtle devoutly hoped that Nancy wasn't going to focus any longer on what made her sad. She quickly said, "Has Whitley been talking about Palmer, maybe? Or arguing with her?"

"I was checking out Palmer's groceries a week ago and Whitley was trying to call her. Palmer was really irritated. She said Whitley could just wait. She was telling the lady she was with that Whitley had been driving her crazy lately. She thought maybe it was her hormones because Whitley is expecting, you know. Palmer said Whitley had been calling her at all hours, dropping by the house, and generally just being a pest."

"Gracious," said Myrtle mildly.

Nancy added, "Palmer said Whitley was suffocating her. I wonder if she broke their friendship off. Maybe Whitley lost it when she did."

"Well, it certainly *could* have happened that way," said Myrtle as she carefully placed the carton of milk in Nancy's cart. She smiled her tremulous old-lady smile at Nancy. "You've been so very kind. I couldn't take up anymore of your time."

Nancy gave her a gentle pat on her arm. "It was my pleasure, Miss Myrtle. I'll walk you over to the checkout. Do you need help getting to your car?"

"Oh, I don't have a car, dear. But Miles kindly drove me over. I told him I was just coming in for the milk so he didn't escort me. Silly of me to leave him in the car. He'll drive up to the front of the store. Besides, the items are easier to handle when they're bagged."

Minutes later, Myrtle walked out of the store, purchases in hand. Miles, as expected, was right at the curb and hurried out to take the bags from her and stow them in his car.

As they drove away, Myrtle said sternly, "You don't have to give me such disapproving looks, Miles. I promise I didn't drive Nancy to tears."

"She was already crying when you saw her in the store?" asked Miles dryly.

"No, but *I* didn't make her upset."

Miles made grumbling noises to indicate that he greatly doubted that.

"Anyway, why did you come inside? Did you need to buy something yourself?"

Miles said, "I wanted to see what was taking you so long. I wondered if maybe there had been an accident on aisle three or something. Once I saw the sobbing Nancy, I realized the issue was the fact that you'd run into another suspect." He paused. "Did you find out anything interesting?"

Myrtle considered this. "I saw that Nancy is very careful with her money. Of course, we realized she wasn't doing well financially when Cash said Nancy had borrowed money from Palmer. Nancy was pulling out coupons and checking them against the weekly store ad—that sort of thing."

"Sounds like a wise course of action."

Myrtle said, "Nancy didn't say anything about Palmer lending her money, but that's a rather personal thing to disclose. Or, perhaps, she was embarrassed by it. She didn't have much of an alibi because she was asleep."

"I doubt the police consider sleeping to be a good alibi," agreed Miles.

"Actually, aside from helping me get my crackers off the floor and exchanged for new ones, she wasn't particularly helpful at all," said Myrtle, a frown creasing her forehead.

"She couldn't offer any ideas on who might have had it in for Palmer?"

Myrtle shrugged. "Well, she thought Palmer wasn't particularly liked in a very *general* way. She did say that Whitley was getting on Palmer's nerves by hovering too much. Nancy guessed that Palmer might have gotten fed up with it and was trying to break off their friendship."

Miles quirked an eyebrow. "And then Whitley, homicidal, followed Palmer out to the diner in the wee hours? Murdered her? It seems rather athletic for an expectant mother."

"Expectant mothers are a lot stronger than you think. Besides, Whitley had other reasons to be upset with Palmer. The fact Palmer was having an affair with her husband, for one."

"Do we think Whitley knew about that?" asked Miles.

"She might have. I was thinking earlier that Whitley seemed awfully upset by Palmer's death to have known about the affair. But maybe it's all a front."

Miles pulled into Myrtle's driveway and reached for the key to turn off the ignition. Myrtle waved him away. "Don't worry with that. We're going to see Wanda."

Miles, however, was resistant. "It's been a busy day, Myrtle. Perhaps we should just go into your house, have a glass of milk, and watch television for a while."

Myrtle shook her head. "Wanda knew I was in danger even before all this started. I want to see if she has more insight for us."

"There are phones," pointed out Miles helpfully. "Perhaps you should just call her. It's such a long drive over there."

Myrtle shot him a look but did pull her phone out of her voluminous purse. She punched Wanda's number in and listened. "There's no answer." She frowned. "Sloan was supposed to replace her broken phone. I wonder if he remembered. I'd have thought he'd have just picked one up at the store and driven it over to her."

"Maybe he did. Maybe she's not answering the phone because she's busy. She's probably outside, tending to her garden."

Myrtle said, "We'll just go over there."

Miles's face fell.

Myrtle scowled at him. "What's the problem? You and Wanda have a good time together. You're always playing virtual chess with her."

"Yes, but that's the point. It's *virtual*. Or perhaps the better way of putting it is *remote* since we're not playing online. She tells me on the phone where she's moved on the board and then I do the same."

"It sounds scintillating, Miles." She sat, waiting for Miles to start driving.

Miles sighed, realizing there was no way out of it, and started the engine again.

As Miles had pointed out, it was always quite a little drive to see Wanda and her irascible brother, Crazy Dan. They lived in a ramshackle shack covered by hubcaps. Crazy Dan occasionally sold one of the hubcaps and then there would be a hole in the middle of them all. The shack was off a highway that had once been a major route but had fallen in popularity since the advent of the interstate decades ago.

When Miles pulled into the driveway, Wanda was already waiting for them outside in a plastic chair. She grinned her gap-toothed smile when she spotted them.

Myrtle hopped out of the car. "Wanda! Glad to see you're all right. We couldn't reach you by phone."

Wanda nodded. "Phone's still broke."

"For heaven's sake. Sloan was supposed to bring you a new one. I swear, these phones aren't worth a dime. While we're here, Miles can take a look at it. He was in IT, after all."

"Engineering," growled Miles.

"Regardless, he knows a lot about how things work," said Myrtle airily.

Wanda led them inside her little house. Miles squared his shoulders and walked in as if he was about to face a firing squad, fingering the bottle of hand sanitizer in the pocket of his khaki pants. Wanda's house was very rarely neat and sometimes inching toward squalid.

But as they entered her home, Miles stopped in surprise. Myrtle did too, blinking. "Mercy! It looks wonderful in here, Wanda. Spring cleaning?"

Wanda blushed a little, looking pleased. "Wasn't just me. Dan helped out some."

"Dan? Has he suffered a mild stroke? You're talking about Dan, your *brother*?"

Wanda nodded. "Reckon he got tired of lookin' at it."

Miles said, "It looks great, Wanda."

She gave him her gap-toothed grin again and handed him her phone. Miles turned on a light (the house, although unusually tidy, was just as dimly-lit as usual) and sat gingerly down in an armchair to study the device. He frowned. "Do you need all these apps?"

Wanda shook her head. "Just need the phone to work."

Myrtle plopped down on a sofa that had seen better days but was covered with a cheerful old quilt. "As you might have imagined, we're here for more than just fixing your phone. I'd like to ask you about your dire message to me."

Wanda bobbed her head. "Yer in danger."

"Yes. I thought it very prescient that you knew about that before Palmer's death."

Miles said dryly, "Well, she is a psychic."

"Yes, but still. Of course, I remember that you also reminded me that the sight works in mysterious ways. But I was wondering if you'd gotten any more glimpses of information that might help me out."

Wanda sighed. "It don't work that way."

"No. But do you know anything about Palmer? Or someone in her circle?"

Wanda, realizing Myrtle was truly scrabbling for clues, sighed again. "Could try to pull out my bits and bobs. Sometimes they work, sometimes they don't."

"Excellent."

Miles glanced up from his work on Wanda's cell phone to see Wanda reaching into a storage container and pulling out a round ball. "Is that a crystal ball?" he asked uneasily.

"Ain't crystal, just glass. Can't afford no crystal."

"Of *course* it's not crystal. Really, Miles," said Myrtle.

Miles asked, "Does it work just as well as crystal?"

Wanda shrugged a thin shoulder. "Sometimes. Sometimes it don't do nuthin' at all."

They quietly watched as Wanda ran a claw-like hand gently over the ball's surface and then looked earnestly into it. Miles and Myrtle saw nothing. Wanda apparently didn't either because after a few minutes, she gave a disgusted sound and then picked up the ball to put it back in its container. As she was closing the plastic lid over it, she stopped short, knitting her eyebrows as she stared at it. Then she breathed in sharply.

"Got something?" asked Myrtle breathlessly.

"Maybe the reception needs to be adjusted," suggested Miles.

Wanda quickly covered up the ball and pushed it away. "Lots of wickedness."

"Anyone in particular, though?" pressed Myrtle. "Perhaps a wicked man? Or a wicked woman?"

Miles sighed.

"I'm just trying to get a lock on the wickedness that's afoot," she answered with a sniff.

Wanda just shook her head. "Both. And bad families."

"Bad families. That sounds very much like *Wuthering Heights*."

Myrtle was about to ask a few more questions when Wanda's gaze fixed on Myrtle's necklace. "That's new."

Myrtle looked down at it, pleased. "Red gave it to me."

"Wear it," croaked Wanda.

"That's the best advice I've heard yet," said Miles.

Wanda looked over at him and said, "Chess? It's yer move."

Miles stood up. "It would be my pleasure. Where's the chess board?"

It was a fair question because Wanda didn't appear to have a dining room or a dining room table. Or, for that matter, a kitchen table. Actually, there were no real flat surfaces around.

"On the floor. Yonder." Wanda bobbed her head toward the back room.

Miles's brow wrinkled in concern. "Crazy Dan isn't back there, is he?"

"Nope. Gone to get bread." Wanda, perhaps sensing Miles's concern, said, "It's jest a laundry room back there."

As Miles disappeared into the laundry room, Wanda said, "Guess you'll be wantin' the horoscope fer Sloan."

"Yes indeed. Are you ready to give it to me?"

"Might as well until it's my turn to play the game," drawled Wanda. They then transitioned into their frequent role of sage and transcriptionist. Wanda's horoscopes, always very direct, were the reason many of the people in Bradley subscribed to the newspaper. She advised Travis that he needed to steer clear of the poison oak patch in his backyard. She informed Wilma that some baby powder would clear up the ant situation in her kitchen.

Myrtle grumbled, "I don't understand why the Sight is so very detailed in one aspect and so unhelpfully vague in another."

Wanda shrugged again. "Don't know."

She continued on until she'd gotten to the end of her prognostic ramblings. Myrtle put the paper away in her purse.

Miles returned, walking stiffly from the laundry room.

Myrtle said, "That must have been a very thoughtful move of yours, Miles. You took quite a long while."

"I couldn't get off the floor," said Miles morosely.

Wanda's voice sounded apologetic. "Sorry 'bout that."

"No trouble. Just let me know your next move when you make it, Wanda."

Myrtle frowned. "How will she manage that if her phone is on the blink?"

"Oh, it's all fixed. Wanda, your storage space on the phone had run out. I just had to eliminate a few things in order to make it work."

She grinned at him, relieved. "Thanks."

# Chapter Thirteen

Minutes later, Myrtle and Miles were back in the car and heading away. Miles said, "Wanda must be a lot more limber than she looks. Getting off the floor isn't easy."

"I have to admit that there are few occasions when I need to get on the floor. I'm not at all sure I would be able to maneuver myself off it when the time came. Was the chess move worth it, at least?"

Miles muttered, "I have the terrible feeling Wanda is about to win the game."

"Well, good for her! Poor thing hasn't had much of a chance to win things over her life. Are you giving yourself a handicap?"

Miles sighed. "No. She's actually really good. Or maybe her Sight is useful for playing chess somehow."

"Maybe she can see herself winning and that gives her the confidence to keep going."

Miles seemed ready to change the subject. "Where are we going now?"

"We should stop by and see Sloan. I need to hand him Wanda's horoscope and talk with him about the story I'm going to write for the paper."

"I'm sure he'll be delighted about that," said Miles.

"As a matter of fact, I think he will. I told him that unless I covered a big story, I was holding my helpful hints column hostage."

Miles frowned. "And that's a good tactic?"

"Apparently, my helpful hints column is the highlight of some poor souls' week. Anyway, I'm going to fill him in on the story I'm working on about Palmer."

"You've been working on a story? When?"

"Oh, it's all in my head right now, but I'll put it on paper soon."

Miles parked on the street in front of the *Bradley Bugle* office and then he and Myrtle walked into the dimly-lit, cluttered newsroom.

As their eyes adjusted to the dark interior, a desk chair wildly squeaked in response. "Miss Myrtle!" said Sloan with a gasp from the other side of the room. And, as something of an afterthought, "And Miles!"

Miles gave him a sympathetic smile. Sloan always found Myrtle so traumatizing.

"Sloan," said Myrtle briskly. "Just wanted to bring you Wanda's horoscopes."

Sloan looked relieved. "Oh good. Thanks for that."

"I also wanted to let you know that Miles was brilliant and fixed Wanda's broken phone."

"Excellent!" Sloan looked cheerful at the prospect of saving a little money.

"*And* I wanted to mention the big story I'm writing for tomorrow's paper."

Sloan crumpled up a little. "Oh."

"It shouldn't come as a surprise, considering that I mentioned on the phone I needed a major article. Then a story fell into my lap."

"Did it?" asked Sloan, looking apprehensive.

"It certainly did. Palmer Baxter's death. Or, rather, her murder."

"Mm."

Myrtle said sternly, "You don't seem very happy about my proposed article."

Sloan hesitated and said, "You might not have seen that we've already covered Palmer's murder in the paper. I wrote the story myself."

"Yes, I did see that. But Sloan, it wasn't much of a story to be perfectly frank. This will be an exclusive and written by someone who was a primary source—me. I was actually on the scene when her tragic death was discovered. What your article lacked was perspective."

Sloan miserably said, "Red's not going to be happy about this."

"Red isn't happy about *anything*. You should know that by now. I'll have my article for you by the end of the day. Oh, and Sloan—you should check your horoscope."

Now Sloan looked even more alarmed than he had earlier. "Wanda mentioned me?"

Myrtle nodded. "Apparently, you should cut back on reckless behavior."

Sloan blushed. "Can't imagine what she's talking about. Maybe I'm speeding a little."

"Well, stop it, whatever it is. Otherwise, you'll end up getting hurt."

Miles hid a smile as Myrtle, ever the high school teacher, scolded her former student once again. He followed her as she left the dim newsroom and walked out into the brightness outside.

They stood there blinking in the unrelenting sunlight. A familiar voice said, "Making mischief, Mama?"

"Red!" said Myrtle. "You just took years off my life. Or however many I might have left, at any rate."

"Sorry, Mama," said Red, looking decidedly unrepentant. "Hi there, Miles. Was Mama dropping off her helpful hints column?"

Myrtle interrupted before Miles could answer. He was a terrible liar, and she had the feeling he would attempt to stumble through an explanation of why they were at the *Bugle*. "As a matter of fact, we were dropping off Wanda's horoscope and telling Sloan all about the big story I'm working on for the paper."

Red glowered at her. "Not on Palmer Baxter."

"*Precisely* on Palmer Baxter. There is no other story in Bradley right now."

Red said, "You're just not looking hard enough. There's Miz Periwinkle at Greener Pastures. She's celebrating her 100th birthday."

Myrtle gave an inelegant snort. "Horsefeathers. If she's a hundred, I'm seventy. She's got to be 105 at the very least. But no one cares after you reach one hundred. Watch her—in another couple of years when everyone's forgotten, she'll celebrate her 100th again."

Miles said, "I guess at that age, you can do whatever you want to. Is she really that old?"

"She most certainly is. She was my Sunday school teacher when I was a child and she wasn't even that young at the time."

"*Anyway*," said Red, "the point is that you can write a story about anything else. I'm getting a very ominous feeling about this particular case, Mama. You need to exercise extreme caution. I don't want you anywhere near it."

"Understood," said Myrtle smoothly. Miles noted that she didn't say she'd follow his directive.

Myrtle continued, "Speaking of the case, how is it all going so far?"

Her son gave her a wary look. "Going fine."

Myrtle said, "I've been thinking about Cash Baxter quite a bit."

"Have you." Miles noted that Red's response was not a question.

"That's right. I took the liberty of looking up the incoming flights to Charlotte for the night in question. It seems to me Cash wouldn't have been on a red-eye flight from Tucson at all. Which does raise a question, don't you think?"

Miles looked at Myrtle with surprise. He wasn't aware that she'd checked on flights at all.

Red's face was annoyed. "This is exactly what I meant when I was talking about you not being involved in all this."

Myrtle just waited, looking expectant.

Red sighed. "As you've already apparently discovered, Cash's alibi isn't very solid. We're working on finding out where he actually was. You wouldn't happen to have any ideas, would you?"

"Why on earth would I know anything?"

"Because you seem to be omnipresent and very possibly omniscient. Everywhere I go and everyone I talk to, it seems they mention having spoken with you." Red frowned at her.

Myrtle shrugged. "They say it's good for the elderly to be social. I have to look after my health, you know."

"And it just happens that the people you're choosing to be social with are my suspects?"

Myrtle's eyes opened wide. "Are they? Gracious! What a treacherous life I lead."

Red said, "Hiram Hudson seemed to be under the mistaken impression that I was taking up golf."

Myrtle demurred. "What are you rambling on about now? Golf? You? You'd burn your skin to death if you spent that much time in the sun. There's just no protection from it on a golf course. Now *Miles* might be interested in taking it up. That could have been why we were over there."

Miles gave Red a meek smile. Red seemed very doubtful about Miles's golfing potential.

Their little tableau on the sidewalk was suddenly interrupted by a cheery bicycle bell.

"Look out," growled Red, swiftly looking around him and appearing to try to use his body to shield Myrtle and Miles.

"Hi there," called out Elaine in a chipper voice. "Look, Jack! It's your Nana and Daddy, too! And Mr. Miles. What a treat!"

Elaine was on the seat of a bicycle and Jack was in an infant seat behind her. He was looking very wary about Elaine's biking abilities. And, judging from what Myrtle knew of Elaine's lack of prowess at all her various hobbies, Myrtle was wary, too.

Red went over and gave Jack a hug. Jack reached his arms up to him, asking to be picked up or, maybe, removed from the possibility of biking altogether. Red gave his son a sympathetic look and ruffled his hair gently. "How has your biking been this morning, Elaine?"

Elaine grinned at him. "Exhilarating! Jack and I must have biked for ten miles already. I'm starving, actually. It's a good thing I brought a backpack with me—Jack and I can bike over to the store and I can pick up some groceries. All this biking is making me want to get some healthy things. Are you up for it, Red?"

Red looked about as wary as Jack did. "I can give it a go. What about Jack, though? He didn't really like our last excursion into healthy eating."

Myrtle remembered it well. Elaine had enthusiastically delved into superfoods. Jack had been less than impressed.

"Jack can be on his usual diet. But I might try to sneak in some more veggies." She turned to Myrtle and Miles. "How are you two doing?"

Miles murmured something pleasant, and Myrtle said, "I suppose we're doing all right. Maybe not quite as well as you and Jack. Is that a new bike? I don't think I remember seeing it at your house before."

Elaine grinned at them. "It's my friend's bike. She bought it some time ago and then got busy with work and hasn't used it. She wants to sell it to me at a special friend rate, but I told her I'd have to try it out and see if I liked it first. I haven't biked since I was a kid."

"They say you never forget," said Miles.

Elaine chuckled. "Yeah, but they leave out the part that you forget a *little*. You still have to perfect the balance and stuff. I didn't realize what a perfect place Bradley was for biking, though. There's that paved path by the lake that's got great views. Plus, there's a greenway. There's not even any traffic here, so the streets are easy to navigate, too."

Red looked as if he devoutly wished Elaine would stay off the streets with the bike.

"Well, do be careful. There are some crazy drivers out there. And you've got precious cargo," said Myrtle.

Jack grinned at his Nana, showing off his pearly-white teeth.

"I will be." Elaine gave another cheerful peal of her bike bell and then wobbled off down the road.

"Heaven help us," breathed Red.

"She seems to at least have control of the bike," said Miles in a comforting voice.

"Does she? I guess she's all right on it. She drives it kind of erratically, though, and people have mentioned that she's taken shortcuts through their yards." Red sighed. "Okay, I've got to head off and meet up with Perkins. Mama, stay out of trouble."

"Tell Perkins hi for me," said Myrtle sweetly as she and Miles headed for the car.

As soon as Miles started up the car, he said, "You didn't mention you'd checked on the Tucson flights. That must have taken a while."

Myrtle said, "What? Oh, that was a bluff. I don't have the patience for that sort of tedious nonsense. I just pretended that I knew Cash didn't have an alibi and waited for Red to confirm it."

"Which he did," said Miles, giving Myrtle an impressed look.

Myrtle shrugged. "It's not such a big deal. I used the same trick when Red was in high school. I'd suspect he was sneaking around doing something he shouldn't do. I'd act all stern and tell him that it was better for him if he just confessed. Then he'd tell me about going to some party instead of being where he said he'd be. It's simply a bluffing tactic I've used before with some success."

When Miles pulled up in front of Myrtle's house she said, "I would invite you in, Miles, but I should get cracking on my story for Sloan. The earlier he gets it in, the easier it will be for him to arrange the front page around it."

"You think it will be a front-page story?"

"Oh, I can ensure that it will be," said Myrtle. Then she added, "It occurs to me that we didn't really get the full breakfast treatment from Bo's Diner, considering the circumstances. Let's go back there tomorrow morning. After all, we were traumatized yesterday and didn't eat much."

Miles muttered, "That's true for me, anyway."

"And oatmeal hardly qualifies as breakfast. We'll have a full breakfast tomorrow—I want to see eggs, bacon, grits, and biscuits on your plate."

Miles looked vaguely ill at the thought. "Sounds like lots of butter and grease."

"It sounds like a southern breakfast. We'll meet up at seven."

The next morning, Myrtle was a little surprised when there was a tap at her door at five-thirty. She looked cautiously out the window, just in case it was a very well-mannered murderer. When she spotted Miles, she swung the door open.

"I figured you'd be up," said Miles simply. He was dressed, as usual, in carefully-pressed khaki pants and a button-down shirt.

"I thought you might be asleep," said Myrtle. "No luck sleeping?"

He shook his head sadly. "None at all. I kept thinking about Palmer."

"It's a good thing we're going to the diner this morning. Maybe it will exorcise the deceased Palmer images from your mind."

Miles sighed. "I hope so. I know she wasn't a very nice person, but she was awfully young to die. And despite her grandstanding, she did seem to do a lot of good things in the town."

"We'll get to the bottom of it, Miles. Did you see my article this morning? Sloan must have stayed up late to get it in."

"Front-page and everything," said Miles, nodding. "The story had a border around it, too."

"It looked very nice," said Myrtle. "Sometimes Sloan gets a little sloppy with his formatting, but I thought he did a good job with that one. Shall we work on some puzzles? I'll get you some coffee."

So the two sat in Myrtle's living room, sipping coffee and working on the crossword and a sudoku. A demanding meow came from outside the front door.

Miles frowned. "Was that Pasha?"

Myrtle quickly walked to the front door. "It sure was. She sounded very persistent. It's a sound I've heard before. Maybe it's about to storm outside or something. I'd better let the poor thing inside."

Myrtle opened the door wide. Which was when Pasha pranced in carrying a small snake.

"Pasha!" gasped Myrtle.

Miles disappeared into the back of the house, returning with a laundry hamper and a broom. "It's just a garter snake," he said calmly.

Pasha gave a mistrustful look to both Miles and the broom. Then she carefully set the snake down on the floor of the living room.

Myrtle said, "She thinks we need to learn how to be better hunters. I'll try to distract her with tuna in the kitchen."

Myrtle opened a can of tuna with as much noise and ceremony as possible in the hopes that Pasha would follow her. But the black cat was intently watching Miles to see how he might handle capturing the snake she'd set free.

Miles lay the hamper on its side and then gently coaxed the snake inside. The snake, naturally, didn't particularly want to enter the hamper. But the alternative was Pasha's jaws, which the snake most certainly didn't want to be held between again. After a moment's hesitation, the snake slithered obediently into the laundry hamper.

"Put it in Erma's yard," said Myrtle with a fair amount of maliciousness. Miles quickly walked outside to let the snake free near the street, deciding that it should just decide where it wanted to go. Then he walked back inside.

"Excellent work, Miles," said Myrtle. "Breakfast this morning is on me."

Miles's brow crinkled. "Don't you have budgetary restraints?"

"Not this morning. I was cleaning up and found ten dollars in an old pair of slacks I was about to give away."

Pasha, clearly disappointed by the lack of bloodshed involved in Miles's approach to hunting, consumed the tuna Myrtle had set out.

Myrtle said, "I suppose Pasha is trying to instruct me in the art of hunting again. She apparently thinks I'm hopeless at it. I thought she'd finally given up, but here we are again."

They resumed their puzzles without further incident until it was time to leave for the diner's seven o' clock opening. Miles's hands gripped the steering wheel tightly as he pulled the car into the parking lot.

"It will be fine, Miles. There aren't even any trucks in the parking lot. It's definitely not a repeat of the last time we were here."

Miles sighed. "I'm having nasty flashbacks, just the same."

"A hearty breakfast will be just the thing to cure those. None of that insipid oatmeal today. Eggs for us both!"

When they walked into the diner, though, there were definitely some similarities to the other day. The staff was huddled grimly and looked startled when Myrtle and Miles entered the restaurant. And, shortly after they walked in, two police cars pulled up into the parking lot.

"Heavens. What's going on?" asked Myrtle.

Bo quickly walked up to Myrtle. "I'm sorry, Miss Myrtle. It seems like we just can't seem to have a normal morning when you're here. Why don't the two of you take a seat and we'll be with you in a few minutes."

Miles started heading obediently to a vinyl booth, but Myrtle put her hands on her hips. "What's going *on*, Bo?"

Bo sighed. "Cash Baxter is dead. One of our servers, Mariah, found him."

# Chapter Fourteen

Mariah, of course, was not only the tearful waitress during their last visit, but Cash's supposed love interest. "She found him?"

Bo nodded. "On her way to her shift here. I don't know much more than that." He turned as the door opened and a couple of state police officers came in. "I'm guessing these guys will fill us in and ask a few questions, too. I'd better run."

Myrtle joined Miles in the booth. "Cash is dead. Apparently, Mariah was the one who discovered him."

Miles nodded. "She's the one who was crying over the ketchup bottles while we were here last time. Where did she find him? It couldn't have been here at the diner, right? There would be emergency vehicles everywhere again."

Myrtle shook her head. "Couldn't have been. Bo said she found him on her way to her shift here. So somewhere on route."

"Outside, then? That seems really strange."

Myrtle said, "We'll have to go visit Mariah and find out what's going on."

Before Miles could lodge an objection at this course of action, their waiter hurried over to them. "Y'all ready to place an order?"

Miles, under the pressure of a deadline, picked up the menu in a panic as Myrtle said, "I'll have the two-egg plate with sausage, cheese grits, and hashbrowns."

Miles said, "I'm going to need a second."

"Why don't you just get the same thing, Miles? It's a little bit of everything."

Miles said, "Because I'll have indigestion if I eat all that this early."

Myrtle said to the waiter, "Let's give him a second. I was wondering if you could help me, actually."

The waiter, a young man with tousled brown hair, looked surprised. "Me?"

"Yes. Bo told me the dreadful news. I know Mariah must be absolutely traumatized. My friend and I would love to bring her something from the diner after we eat here. Do you know what her favorite selection is?"

Miles frowned at Myrtle.

The young waiter grinned at them. "Well, sure. That's nice of you. Mariah always eats the lumberjack breakfast."

Myrtle said, "A delicious choice. I often get that, myself. Could you add that as a to-go order for us?"

The waiter jotted it down on his order pad. "And you, sir?"

Miles looked vaguely unsure of himself, as he always did when placing an order. "I'd like a scrambled egg and some toast. Wheat bread."

Myrtle made a face as the waiter added it to the orders. "Be back in a jiffy," he said as he walked away.

"I'm not very hungry," said Miles in defense of his order. "I have the feeling if I put too much on my stomach, it's going to revolt."

"You have such delicate organs," said Myrtle. "One day, I want to see you order something robust from the menu. Like the lumberjack breakfast."

"I wasn't a lumberjack," mumbled Miles.

"But 'accountant breakfast' doesn't have quite the same ring to it," said Myrtle.

Miles sighed.

"Anyway, what do we think about Cash's untimely demise? This is all getting out of hand. First Palmer and then her husband? Plus, it's most annoying having our prime suspect become a victim. After hearing that Cash's alibi was no good, I was planning on asking him a few questions."

"I suppose Cash must have known something about who killed Palmer. Or maybe he *thought* he knew and asked a few too many questions of the wrong person." Miles paused. "Are we really going to go see Mariah?"

"We certainly are. I'm going to get the waiter to give me her address just as soon as he comes back over."

But the waiter didn't know Mariah's address, not exactly. He only knew that she lived in a small house with her roommate.

"Enjoy your meals," said the young man as he hurried off to another table.

"I'll send Bitsy a text and get the address," said Myrtle as she reached for her phone.

"If Bitsy checks her messages."

Myrtle said, "Oh, Bitsy is on top of things."

Sure enough, Myrtle had just sent the inquiring text when her phone started ringing in response.

"Miss Myrtle. I'm glad you texted me. Mariah is in a real state."

"Well, of course she is. Bless her heart. It must all be very upsetting."

Bitsy answered, "It sure is. The problem is, I have to get to work. I was feeling pretty awful about leaving her alone."

"Don't you worry. Miles and I are just finishing up here at the diner and we'll be over shortly with her favorite breakfast."

Bitsy said, "You're an angel, Miss Myrtle." She gave Myrtle their address.

Her voice carried over to Miles, who was just starting to eat, despite Myrtle's verdict that they were finishing up. He made a face.

Myrtle hung up the phone and said, "Now we're in good shape. Except that you should probably chew a little faster. You don't eat as quickly as I do."

Miles picked up his wheat toast and took an unenthusiastic bite. "I'm sure Mariah won't be completely on her own when Bitsy leaves. There must be cops all over the place."

"Well, let's just try to leave quickly."

With Myrtle's coaching, Miles was able to finish his scrambled egg and toast in record time. Myrtle, as usual, eliminated everything on her place in mere minutes and waited as patiently as she possibly could while Miles thoughtfully chewed his toast. For Miles, however, it was practically as if he were gobbling it down.

Myrtle paid for their breakfast and the take-out and then they headed for Miles's car.

"Where is this house?" asked Miles.

"Not far from here. I'll direct you."

Unfortunately, however, Myrtle's sense of direction was not particularly good that morning. They ended up on an unpaved dead-end road near the lake.

"This doesn't seem right," said Miles.

Myrtle scowled at the road in front of them. "This *should* be right."

"Perhaps we should use technology for once. Put the address into your phone."

Myrtle scowled even more. "I rarely use that GPS app. After all, I'm always in Bradley. I've resided here for over eighty years. I know practically every nook and cranny in the place."

"Except for this one." Miles pulled out his own phone and, tapping its sleek surface, summoned his maps app. "What's the address?"

After Myrtle provided it for him, a polite digital voice directed them to a location quite opposite from the one they were currently in. When they arrived, they saw that there were still emergency vehicles there. Fortunately, Red had apparently already left the scene.

Miles looked suddenly mulish. "Doesn't it seem rather intrusive? We really don't know Mariah."

"She'll appreciate the gesture," said Myrtle in a confident manner. "Besides, she's probably barely thinking straight right now, considering." She climbed out of the car bearing the take-out bag.

Miles hesitated. "There's still crime-scene tape outside the house."

Myrtle said, "So the police are still going through everything inside. Mariah must be somewhere outside."

They looked around and saw the young woman slumped in the backseat of a police car. When she spotted Myrtle and Miles, a look of surprise crossed her features. Then she gave them an uncertain wave.

"Bitsy must not have told her we were coming by," said Miles with a sigh as they headed in the direction of the police car. "It all would have been much easier if she had."

Myrtle said briskly, "Bitsy was probably being questioned separately by the police and couldn't tell her. It'll be fine. The poor thing must be starving by now."

And, actually, Mariah was hungry. When she caught sight of the Bo's Diner bag and learned that Myrtle and Miles were bringing it to her, she burst into tears.

Once Mariah had cried herself out (in fairly short order, Myrtle was pleased to see), Myrtle plied her with coffee and food. Mariah, in just a few more minutes, seemed much more in control of herself.

"You've been very sweet to me," said Mariah. "I appreciate it."

"Well, it just so happened that Miles and I were at the diner again this morning. The staff was all very concerned about you."

Mariah nodded. "Bo told me not to even try to come in—just to take the day off. He called in somebody else to cover for me."

"Very kind of Bo. How are you holding up?"

Mariah blinked the tears away and set her jaw. "I'll be okay. Better than Cash, anyhow."

"Yes. About Cash . . . I couldn't help but see that the police seem to be spending a good deal of time inside your house. That seemed a bit unusual, from what I've been able to observe of police investigations. My son, you know, is Red."

Mariah's glistening eyes opened larger. "Oh. I'd forgotten that." She paused, as if mulling something over. Then she said, "You know, I might as well say. It's gonna be all over Bradley by lunchtime. I was . . . seeing Cash."

Myrtle said briskly, "I rather thought so, my dear. And I know you must be very upset about what happened. Just know that Miles and I are here to help you in any way that we can. We want to figure out who's behind these deaths so that innocent people aren't under suspicion."

"You think I'm innocent?" asked Mariah in a somewhat desperate way.

"Well, I don't think Bitsy, an eminently practical person, would choose to live with a murderer."

Mariah said, "No, you're right. Bitsy is so smart. There's no way she'd put herself in a bad place." She paused again. "Okay, I'm going to fill you in. I hope you won't think too badly of me."

"Of course I won't," said Myrtle smoothly.

Mariah took a deep breath. "Like I said, I was seeing Cash. I didn't feel very good about it, since he was married and everything. He told me that Palmer was seeing somebody else, too, and that they didn't have a real marriage—I mean, like traditional. I guess I sort of fell for him. I wasn't acting like myself." She looked at Myrtle and Miles then. Her face was flushed. "I feel kinda embarrassed talking to you two this way. You're seniors and all. You probably think I was so dumb."

"Not at all. Miles and I have lived a long time and nothing surprises us."

Mariah nodded. "Okay. Well anyway, I was heading to my early shift at the diner." She pointed to the uniform she was still wearing. "When I walked outside, I saw Cash's car was still on the street outside my house."

Miles cleared his throat. "I'm guessing that was unusual."

"Oh, yes. Cash would leave at 4:30 in the morning before anyone got up. I walked closer to see if he was still sitting in his car. I thought maybe he'd fallen asleep or something. That's when I saw him on the ground."

Mariah's voice broke and Myrtle quickly interrupted to refocus her and keep the tears at bay. "Could you tell how he'd been attacked?"

Mariah shook her head. "Not at first. But then I went over to make sure I couldn't help him in some way—call an ambulance or something. There wasn't any blood around him, but I could tell he was dead." She crossed herself.

Myrtle said, "Did Cash seem preoccupied with anything? Was he worried about somebody or something, that you could tell?"

"He did seem that way. It was like he was with me, but he wasn't *with* me, you know? I was starting to wonder if he was cheating on me with somebody else."

Myrtle asked, "Did you have any proof of that? Text messages, spurious phone calls, lipstick on his collar? That sort of thing?"

"No. It was just that his mind was somewhere else. And he didn't sleep well . . . he was tossing and turning a lot. He was really secretive, too. He used to tell me all sorts of things but then he got all quiet after Palmer's death."

Miles said, "I might have thought he was responsible for Palmer's death. If he started acting that way, I mean."

Mariah nodded. "Yeah, I would have too, except I knew he didn't do it. See, he wasn't on an airplane when Palmer was murdered. He was with me."

"I see," said Myrtle. "So you were his alibi."

"Yes. But I guess he was being a gentleman and didn't want to pull me into things—he didn't tell the cops that he was with me. Instead, he made up something about his flight on the spur of the moment. Then he kept doubling-down on the lie about the flight, even though the cops had checked his alibi and found out he wasn't telling the truth. I was about to talk to Red to let him know the truth when this happened."

A police officer came by the car and said, "You can go back into the house, miss."

"Thanks," she answered, sounding distracted. She looked at Myrtle and Miles. "I don't even think I had anything in the house to eat this morning and I didn't want to get into Bitsy's food. I really appreciate it."

"Think no more about it," said Myrtle. "Miles and I were happy to help out. And please take care. Let me know if you need anything."

Miles was looking leerily at the spot where Cash had died and jumped slightly when his name was mentioned. He and Myrtle walked back to his car.

"Well," said Myrtle as she put on her seatbelt. "That was something."

Miles edged away from the curb and started driving in the direction of downtown. "We're heading home, I suppose?"

"What? No, I don't think so, Miles. We should go see Shay."

Miles looked mulish. "Myrtle, it's still very early in the day. Some people don't rise as early as we do."

"Working people do. And Shay is a worker. Besides, even if it's her day off, she'll be up by now. I guarantee you Red has already paid her a visit. They'll be searching Cash's house for any clues as to why he was murdered. And he'll probably want to know exactly where Shay was since she's a likely suspect."

Miles frowned. "Why is Shay a suspect again? She seems like the meek and nonviolent type. Plus, isn't she benefitting from the situation? After all, she's living on Palmer's and Cash's property."

"Except there's the matter of the will Shay let us read."

Miles said, "Ahh. Right, the will."

"The way Palmer wrote her will, Shay would be the beneficiary if Cash pre-deceased her. The bulk of the fortune was Palmer's, after all. And, of course, the will hasn't even gone through probate yet. Shay is going to be a wealthy woman."

"I suppose she can adopt all the dogs and cats she wants now," mused Miles.

"Indeed, she can."

Miles knit his brows. "I still say it's quite early for a social visit. Shouldn't we bring along food or something?"

Myrtle snapped her fingers. "I meant to pick up an extra to-go order for Shay from the diner. For heaven's sake. I suppose I could run by the house and whip up a quick casserole or something."

Miles quickly said, "You know what might be better? Comfort food?"

"Yes. Casseroles qualify."

Miles said, "So do chocolate chip cookies. I picked up a batch from the Piggly Wiggly deli and they were absolutely delicious. Chewy, with big chunks of chocolate in them."

Myrtle looked doubtful. "That's not really a traditional Southern bereavement food."

"Sometimes you need to shake things up a little. The grocery store is open, and we can slide by it on the way to the Baxter estate."

Miles looked relieved when Myrtle finally, reluctantly agreed.

Minutes later, cookies in tow, they drove over to see Shay. As Myrtle had expected, there were several police cars there. One of them was Red's sedan. Red was standing next to it, speaking with Lieutenant Perkins. He narrowed his eyes as he spotted Miles's car pull in through the gates to the property.

"He doesn't look happy," Miles observed.

"Oh, he's never happy. I don't know when he got so cranky. He used to be very easy-going when he was a youngster." Myrtle blithely waved at Red who strode over.

"Just keep driving," said Myrtle. "Pretend you don't see him."

"Sorry, I pull over when cops tell me to." Miles carefully slowed the car to a stop.

# Chapter Fifteen

Myrtle heaved a big sigh as Red gestured for her to roll down her window. Then she said in a perky tone, "Good morning, Red. Nice to see you today. Miles and I are bringing some cookies to Shay. The poor thing has lost all her remaining family in the last few days."

Red glowered at her. "If I didn't know better, Mama, I'd think you had a police scanner at your house."

"What a silly thing to say! I wouldn't want to listen to all that nonsense. Half of it would be reports from Maylene Merriweather saying kids were cutting through her yard on the way to the creek. No, Miles and I were at the diner having an early breakfast when we heard the news."

Lieutenant Perkins walked over and stood next to Red. "Good morning, Mrs. Clover."

She beamed at him. "Good morning to you!"

Red said to Perkins, "She's heading over to talk with Shay Cunningham." Red's displeasure was evident from his tone.

Perkins smiled at Myrtle. "If I know you, you're bringing some sort of food along with you."

Myrtle nodded, looking sad. "Miles and I were so sorry to hear that Shay had sustained yet another loss. The poor thing has had such a troubled life that it doesn't seem quite fair she's having to deal with more problems. We've got some cookies with us and are planning to see how she's holding up."

Red said, "I can report she's holding up just as well as can be expected. And I'd be happy to deliver the cookies to Shay."

He suddenly looked both suspicious and dismayed. "They're not homemade, are they?"

"What a peculiar question! They *would* have been homemade, but Miles insisted that he'd recently purchased excellent cookies from the Piggly Wiggly."

Red and Miles exchanged glances and Red gave Miles a respectful nod.

Perkins said, "Well, I'm sure Ms. Cunningham will be very grateful. We're all done speaking with her, I believe?" He gave Red a questioning look.

Red gave an exasperated sigh. "I guess so. But Mama, stop sticking your nose in where it doesn't belong. We've had two mysterious deaths now. I sure don't want you to be the third."

And with that cheerful statement, Red backed away from the car and allowed them to drive toward Shay's cottage.

When Shay opened the door, she looked pale and shaken. But Myrtle was relieved to note that she didn't burst into tears this time. "Y'all are too kind," she said. "Please come inside."

"Are you sure?" asked Miles, ignoring Myrtle's side-eye. "We know it's been an awful day already."

"You'll be making things better if you join me," said Shay. "I don't think I can stand being by myself right now."

They followed her into the cottage, which looked much changed from the last time they'd been there. There were now boxes and bags everywhere. There was packing tape, bubble wrap, and newspapers on the floor. All sorts of possessions seemed to be shoved, willy-nilly, into the various containers.

"Gracious," said Myrtle. "What happened here?"

Shay looked sadly around her. "It's a mess, isn't it? I'm sorry. Miles, if you could just put those things on the floor there should be room on the sofa for you both."

Miles carefully removed the pots and pans and kitchen tools from the sofa and he and Myrtle gingerly sat down.

Shay had a completely overwhelmed look on her face. "I don't even know where to start."

"How about if you start with a cookie?" said Myrtle, still hoping tears weren't on the forecast. "A little sugar might do you some good."

Shay opened up the box of cookies and unenthusiastically took a bite. Then her eyes brightened. "These are good."

Miles gave a smug nod.

Myrtle rose from the sofa and brought Shay a glass of milk.

A few minutes later, looking a bit better, Shay said, "Thank you. I guess I needed a little food this morning. With everything going on, I'd totally forgotten to eat."

Myrtle said, "I can only imagine. I suppose the police were here earlier than we were."

Shay nodded. "I was up early, though, so it wasn't like they woke me up. I was trying to get some packing done before work. After the police told me about Cash, though, I asked for the day off. There's no way I'd have been worth anything today. My head feels like it's swimming."

Miles cleared his throat. "About the packing. You were moving? Locally?"

Shay rubbed a hand absently against the side of her face. "Well, I was trying to. I didn't have a place to *go* yet, but I was at least trying to put my stuff together."

"Why is that?" asked Myrtle. "I was given to understand that you liked being here and that your lodgings were complimentary."

Shay nodded. "They were. But Cash asked me to go."

"What on earth for? Didn't he realize you don't have a place to move to?"

Shay sighed. "I don't think it even occurred to Cash. He's lived with money for a while, and I guess he didn't even think about not having enough money to move. I do have some savings I've built up, but I was hoping to use those to get medical stuff done. I don't have medical insurance, you know."

It all sounded like the most tremendous mess to Myrtle. "Did Cash give you any reason why he wanted you to move out?"

"Not really. But then, I kind of understood. After all, it was Palmer who was hosting me. With Palmer gone, maybe Cash wanted the whole property to himself. Or maybe he wanted to get it ready to sell. He could leave town and work somewhere else—somewhere he didn't have so many memories of Palmer. He had his reasons and that was good enough for me. I went and collected empty boxes out behind the grocery store and started packing my things."

"That's awfully understanding of you," said Miles.

"Yes," agreed Myrtle. "Tell me—what did you think of Cash? What was he like? I don't feel as if I knew him very well."

Shay sighed again. "I don't like speaking ill of the dead, of course."

"Nobody does, dear."

Encouraged, Shay continued, "He was fine, really. I never felt like I knew him, though. He kept his feelings hidden. And his face didn't show much."

Myrtle nodded. "He had a façade."

Shay nodded uncertainly. "I guess. But after Palmer died, I walked over to the house to see if I could help him out at all. This was right before he asked me to move. He jumped half a mile when I started talking. Said I was sneaking up on him. I could tell he had a lot on his mind."

Myrtle said, "When you spoke with the police, did they mention anything about Cash having an affair?"

"They did. They told me he was at the woman's house when he died."

Miles said, "You don't sound very surprised at that."

Shay shook her head. "Not really. Their marriage wasn't all that great. But I felt like that wasn't the only thing he was hiding. Maybe he knew what happened to Palmer. He could have found out while he was clearing out her things. Maybe Palmer kept a love note or had a personal calendar or something." She lowered her voice as if someone could hear her from outside the cottage.

"Have you thought further on who might be responsible for Palmer's death?"

Shay paused. "Well, the more I think about it, the more I believe Nancy might have been desperate enough to do something. I know a little about desperation myself, and I can understand how she might have felt."

Myrtle thought back to being at the grocery store and Nancy's careful calculations to work out what she could afford to buy. "I can imagine that, too."

"Maybe Palmer was really putting pressure on her. I know she was getting annoyed with Nancy."

"She told you that?" asked Myrtle.

"I was actually there when Palmer was on the phone with Nancy," said Shay. "I couldn't hear what Nancy was saying on her end, but whatever it was, Palmer was furious. She kept saying that Nancy 'should have thought about that' and that she didn't want to hear from Nancy unless she was calling to say a check was in the mail."

"And what did you think Palmer meant when she said Nancy should have thought things through?"

Shay said, "Well, that Nancy should have been prepared to pay her back." She was quiet for a moment. "Don't get me wrong—Palmer could be super-generous. You know how she put me through rehab, set me up in a house, and helped get me a job. But I guess I was family and she had different expectations. After all, there was no way I could ever have afforded to pay Palmer back for everything she did for me. And there was no expectation that I ever needed to. It was a gift."

"One that Cash apparently didn't feel like continuing to bestow," said Myrtle.

Shay sighed. "Yeah. I mean, I got it. I was sorry about it, and I didn't totally understand why he was doing it, but I knew I wasn't kin to Cash. Anyway, in regard to Nancy, I guess Palmer looked at it as more of a business transaction, you know? She wanted to help Nancy, but she didn't want to lose any money in the process, either."

Myrtle said, "Well, she certainly seemed to be very effective in business. Everything she did was very organized." She looked at her watch. "Miles, you and I should probably be heading out. It was lovely to see you Shay . . . we're just sorry about the circumstances."

Shay walked out with them, carefully locking the door to the house behind her. "Thanks so much for coming by and for the cookies. I'm going to be enjoying those as I set about unpacking." She hesitated. "Could y'all do me a favor? Nobody else knew Cash asked me to leave the cottage. Besides the cops, I mean . . . they saw the boxes, too. Could y'all keep that under your hat? It'll make me look so petty if word gets out about him asking me to leave when Cash has just passed away."

"Of course we will," said Myrtle. Miles nodded.

"Thanks again," she said with a smile. She waved as they set off in the car out of the long driveway and through the gates to the street outside.

# Chapter Sixteen

"Back to your house?" asked Miles hopefully.

"Yes, let's shore up with some more coffee and maybe take a few minutes to think and plan our next move. What did you make of all that, Miles?"

Miles said, "That Cash and Palmer weren't very nice people."

"No, they certainly weren't. Still, there are ways of handling people that aren't very nice. One could upbraid them at book club or demote them at work. One could simply cross to the other side of the street when spotting them. Murdering them seems unnecessary. Plus, they were young people. Perhaps they might have improved with age like a fine wine."

"Not everything improves with age," noted Miles.

"Agreed. Still, I think we can both agree that, on principle, Palmer and Cash shouldn't have endured violent deaths at the hands of some ghastly perpetrator. Shay seemed to think Nancy might have been involved in all this."

Miles said, "You spent all that time with Nancy in the grocery store. What did you make of her?"

"She seems like a very calm, rational person. But then, she was dealing with me and not with Palmer. I can picture her feeling very desperate and wanting to do something to make her situation better. Still, Palmer did behave rather kindly to Nancy, if you think of it."

Miles raised his eyebrows. "By pressuring Nancy to pay her back? By telling people that Nancy had borrowed money and wasn't paying on schedule?"

"By lending her money in the first place. A bank wouldn't have done it—they'd have realized she was a poor prospect for paying them back. And Nancy mentioned that Palmer had helped her get the job at the Piggly Wiggly."

Miles was thoughtful. "That was fairly kind, actually."

"Yes. There was that side to Palmer. But there was, also, a competing mean side, I believe."

Miles pulled into Myrtle's driveway and said, "Uh-oh."

Myrtle frowned and followed his gaze. "For heaven's sake."

Red was standing on Myrtle's little front porch. He turned and waved, looking rather grim, as he heard Miles's car.

Miles said, "Maybe I should just head home for a little while."

"Certainly not! That's not what we planned. You'll come in and have coffee." It was less an invitation than a command.

Myrtle swept out of the car and down her front walkway. "Red. What a surprise."

"Hi, Mama," said Red, frowning. "Have a nice visit with Shay?"

"I did, as a matter of fact. She was delighted to have cookies and a chat. Speaking of Shay, shouldn't you be scouring the countryside for whomever killed her cousin? And Cash?"

She opened her front door and walked in, holding it for Red and the reluctant Miles.

Red drawled, "It's lunchtime. I decided to run back home for a quick sandwich. That's when Erma intercepted me. She told me that she'd seen you biking down the street."

Miles made a strangled sound.

Myrtle erupted. "What? Erma must have been getting into her cooking sherry. Of *course* I'm not riding a bike. I'm not suicidal, Red, regardless of what you might think. For heaven's sake."

Red sighed. "I know. She sounded so sure, though. I thought maybe you'd been inspired by Elaine's biking adventures."

"Perhaps Erma needs glasses. She most likely saw Elaine and not me."

Red frowned as if trying to picture how Erma could have confused his lithe wife with his octogenarian mother. "Maybe she does. Anyway, now that I've satisfied myself that she was very mistaken, I'll be on my way."

"No you won't. It's a good thing you're here, Red. As it happens, I have a leaky faucet in my bathroom. I'd like it to be fixed."

Red closed his eyes briefly. "I'm working a homicide, Mama."

"As you said yourself, you're on a lunch break. I'll make you a sandwich while you work."

Red looked as if he might continue to argue.

"If my water bill is too high," said Myrtle sweetly, "I might not be able to pay it. Then I'd have my water turned off and would have to move in with you, Elaine, and Jack for a while until I can afford to have the service started up again."

Red headed back toward the bathroom. He absently set his phone down as he did.

As soon as he was out of sight, Myrtle immediately picked it up.

Miles's eyes were huge. "What are you doing?" he hissed.

"Getting Perkins's phone number off Red's phone," murmured Myrtle. "I tried calling his old number a few times lately and he's apparently changed numbers."

"You're going to get caught." Miles looked anxiously toward the back.

But Myrtle was already scrolling through Red's contacts. When she came across the Lieutenant's number, she carefully wrote it down on a notepad. Then she hurried to the kitchen to make a peanut butter and jelly sandwich as sounds of clanging metal and muttered curses came from the bathroom.

There was a resounding crash and then the curses were no longer simply muttered. Miles looked at Myrtle with concern.

She shrugged. "He's clearly not unconscious."

A few minutes later, Red came back out, face flushed. He was rubbing his head with one hand. "Your leaky faucet is fixed," he growled.

"Wonderful!" said Myrtle. "Happy day. Did something happen back there? I thought I heard a noise."

"I slipped and hit my head." Red's voice was sulky.

"Goodness. Perhaps you need a medic alert necklace, yourself. I believe they have different types for gentlemen. One you can attach to your belt, even."

Red shot her a look.

Myrtle continued cheerfully, "I made you a sandwich. I even scrounged up some chips from somewhere in the pantry. It's hard to keep chips here, you know. Puddin usually gets into them."

Red sighed. "I've gotta take it to-go, Mama. I think I've just about used up all my time with this plumbing escapade." He quickly wrapped the sandwich in a paper towel and dumped the small collection of chips into a napkin. "See you both later." And he quickly made his escape.

Miles finally breathed again. "That was close, Myrtle."

"It wasn't at all close. You just have a tough time doing something furtive. It's all fine. Now I get to call Lieutenant Perkins on the phone. He can be hard to catch up with during an investigation, you know. This way I can talk to him whenever I want. We can share information—or trade it."

Miles looked doubtful "Do you think he'll engage like that? Over the phone, I mean. It seems like the police have to be pretty closed-mouthed when they're working on a case. Particularly a murder case."

"Well, he's my best bet, anyway. He's always extremely polite and respectful. If he *can't* say something, he'll very carefully let me know. In fact, I believe I'll call him up right now. After all, we know Red isn't with him, so it'll be the perfect time."

She carefully dialed his number while Miles looked somewhat anxious.

Perkins picked up right away. "Mrs. Clover. Is everything all right?"

"Oh, everything is fine on my end. But Miles and I have been fretting about things and I thought it might help me sleep better if you relieved my mind on one point."

Perkins said in his deferential manner, "I'm so sorry you've been worried about the case. What's been on your mind? I'll help you if I can."

"Well, the diner has a special place in my heart. I grew up going there and have seen generations of the family work there. I would just hate it if Bo was arrested for murder and the diner had to change hands."

Miles gave her an approving look at the topic she'd chosen to bring up with Perkins.

Perkins said, "I'm happy to let you know that at least five individuals could attest that Bo was focused on food preparation and didn't leave their sight the entire time. I hope that information will help you sleep a little better, Mrs. Clover."

"I'm afraid my sleep is a lost cause but perhaps I might get a few more winks now. Thank you, Lieutenant Perkins."

Myrtle hung up and smiled at Miles. "More diner days ahead of us. But for now, I think we should put together something to eat, ourselves. I actually have something better than the peanut butter I gave Red. And I have better chips, too."

Several minutes later, Myrtle and Miles had a feast of tomato sandwiches, barbeque potato chips, and red grapes.

"I think we should spoil ourselves and eat while watching television," said Myrtle. "They always say not to do that, but I feel rather rebellious today."

"I've noticed," said Miles dryly.

So the rest of the afternoon was spent with good food, good company, and several excellent television shows, back-to-back.

# Chapter Seventeen

Taking an afternoon and evening off made Myrtle relaxed, but it also made her wake up the next morning raring to get started on the case. She called Miles at around eight. "You sound alert this morning," said Myrtle.

"I got a full night's sleep for once. What's the plan for to-day?"

"I think it's probably time to speak with Hiram again. Then maybe we can run by and see Whitley. They were close friends with both Cash and Palmer and I think they can give us more information on those two."

Miles said, "When would you like to head out?"

"How about fifteen minutes from now?"

Miles quickly said, "Isn't it awfully early for a social visit?"

"Oh, it won't be a social visit. We'll head over to the country club and visit Hiram in the pro shop again."

Miles said, "I thought Red made it very clear to Hiram that he doesn't plan on taking up golf. That was your previous excuse for being there. Do you have a new one?"

"Don't be so obstructive, Miles! I'll say that I'm still trying to persuade him—that he needs to take up some gentle exercise for his health. Besides, Hiram is always delighted to see me. I was his favorite teacher. See you in fifteen minutes."

Sure enough, fifteen minutes later, Myrtle and Miles were on their way to the country club. The weather was rather threatening. The sky was the brightest of blues but the clouds spotting it were a violent black. It was the kind of weather they saw during summer afternoons, not early in the day.

"Looks like a thunderstorm," said Miles gloomily as he parked the car. "Maybe we should bring the umbrellas in."

"The forecast this morning said that the storms would hold off until lunchtime. At least this way we know there won't be many golfers vying for Hiram's attention."

Hiram was, indeed, by himself in the pro shop. He was straightening up already-straight merchandise and looked relieved when the bell on the door rang to indicate customers had come in.

He blinked in surprise to see Myrtle and Miles there.

"Miss Myrtle! Miles. How are you today?"

Myrtle bestowed her sweetest of smiles on him. "We're doing well, Hiram. I thought we'd pop by and take a look at some of your merchandise here."

Hiram hesitated. "I hate to discourage you, Miss Myrtle, but Red came by and said he wasn't interested in doing any golfing."

Myrtle said, "I know he doesn't *want* to, but he needs to take up some gentle exercise, according to his doctor. That's the thing about Red and me—we look after each other. He got me this lovely medic alert necklace. I'm going to try and help him lower his blood pressure. That's what family does."

Hiram said, "You're a great mom. Have a look around the shop and let me know if you have any questions."

"I sure will."

Myrtle started perusing the various items in the store. Her eyebrows immediately went up. Miles gave a wry smile.

"Heavens!" she hissed at Miles. "These clubs are seven-hundred dollars."

"Those are irons, I believe," said Miles helpfully.

"And those over there are three-hundred."

"Drivers," identified Miles. "Maybe you should just shop the clothing. They have golf shirts over there."

Myrtle strode over to study the golf shirts. They seemed awfully preppy for Red who was either in police uniform or wore tee-shirts and shorts. "These seem rather pricey, too."

The phone rang and Hiram got on a call with a golfer who was trying to reserve a tee time. Myrtle continued shopping, a horrified expression on her face at the price of each bit of merchandise.

"Why don't you just pick up some golf balls? This is just an excuse for talking with Hiram, anyway."

"You think so? I believe those are the only things in the shop I can afford." Myrtle picked up a box of golf balls and headed to the register just as Hiram was wrapping up his phone call.

"Here we are," said Myrtle cheerfully. "Some golf balls for Red."

Hiram looked confused. "I thought Red mentioned that he didn't have any clubs."

Myrtle gave him a big, old-lady smile. "Oh, I found a club in the thrift store."

Miles closed his eyes briefly.

"A club? What type?" asked Hiram.

Myrtle waved her hands airily. "The kind you hit golf balls with. Really, I have no idea. Anyway, he'll be able to practice with the balls here."

Hiram apparently realized he wasn't going to get any further asking questions and started ringing up the purchase.

Myrtle said, "I wanted to tell you, also, how sorry I am about Cash Baxter. I know the two of you were friends. How awful this must be for you."

Hiram suddenly looked sober. "Yes. I couldn't believe it when I heard the news. I didn't have an opening shift, so I slept in a little. I needed the sleep too, because poor Whitley has been tossing and turning all night. She just can't seem to get comfortable."

"It must be difficult to get situated when you're about to deliver a baby. I suppose it was the same for me—it was just so very long ago that I can't remember."

Hiram nodded. "Whitley's been having a hard time. Anyway, I didn't find out what had happened to Cash until later in the morning."

Myrtle said, "I'm sure it was very difficult news to hear. The whole situation is just so sad. Both Palmer and Cash, young people in their prime, struck down within a week's time." She shook her head sorrowfully. "And all of these unsavory details coming out about their marriage. It's all such a pity."

"Unsavory details?" Hiram's expression was interested.

"Yes. Well, Cash was seeing someone else, just as Palmer was. Did Cash confide in you about that?"

Hiram sighed. "I didn't realize it for a long while. But then I learned about it a few weeks ago. I didn't get the impression his relationship with Mariah was anything Cash was proud of or that he wanted for the long-term. I only found out because I overheard a phone conversation between Cash and Mariah and asked him about it. It wasn't something he wanted to talk about."

Myrtle nodded. "I'm sure he didn't. I was wondering if Cash seemed different lately . . . was something on his mind? I've been trying to think why someone would have felt they needed to murder him and coming up a little short."

Hiram shook his head, looking abashed. "I haven't actually spoken to Cash since Palmer died."

"Oh?"

Hiram sighed. "I'm just awful at that kind of thing, Miss Myrtle. I figured Cash would be cut up about Palmer's death. Even though they didn't always get along, I know Cash cared for Palmer. He always said he really respected her drive." He said, "I know it sounds terrible that I didn't call him up. Whitley, did, though. She drove over to his house with some blueberry muffins she'd made."

"Did Whitley tell you how he was doing?"

Hiram shook his head. "She said he was very polite, but didn't say anything but the pleasantries. He took the muffins, thanked her, and then headed back inside."

"Who do you think was responsible for Cash's death? Do you have any ideas?"

Hiram shrugged helplessly. "Maybe different people killed Palmer and Cash. Maybe Mariah got wind of the fact Cash was planning on dumping her. When I found out about the affair a few weeks ago, Cash mentioned that he was planning on ending the relationship and trying to get more of a handle on his life. He even talked about hiring a life coach to help him sort it all out."

"A life coach? In Bradley?" asked Myrtle.

"They were going to be virtual sessions. Anyway, Cash felt like nothing was going right for him, personally. Ending his relationship with Mariah was high on the list. She could have flown into a rage and killed him. Maybe she even killed Palmer, thinking Cash would marry her if Palmer wasn't around. It's hard to know what goes through people's heads." He paused for a second. "Do you know how Cash died?"

Myrtle shook her head. "Just that it happened."

Hiram said thoughtfully, "Shay is also a possibility. I guess the whole property and money will go to her now. Since she didn't have anything, and I mean *anything*, before, I'd guess the police are paying a lot of attention to her right now. Money is a powerful motive."

Myrtle nodded. "It certainly is. Well, Miles and I should get going. Thanks for talk, Hiram."

He gave her a friendly smile. "Thanks for coming by."

Miles said, "That was very interesting. It sounds like Cash was considering having a complete life makeover."

"I don't totally understand what life coaches do," said Myrtle.

"Well, from what I've read, they help their clients with the areas of their lives that they want to overhaul. I guess they give them homework and whatnot. It helps them to look at everything from a global view and decide what changes they want to implement."

Myrtle frowned. "So maybe Cash was considering another line of work?"

"Maybe. Or maybe he wanted to overhaul everything in his life—perhaps he was even thinking about undergoing marriage counseling with Palmer."

"Hmm," said Myrtle.

"What are you thinking now? You'd mentioned seeing Whitley. I'm not totally sure how you're going to make that work, though. We've already used the baby toy ploy. Is there another trumped-up reason you can come up with why we might need to visit her? That's plausible?"

Miles put a lot of emphasis on "plausible."

Myrtle frowned. "Wait. When is Palmer's funeral? I think I've lost track of time."

"Considering how quickly they like to bury the dead here, I'm sure it's coming up soon." He paused.

"Tippy will know," said Myrtle decisively.

Tippy picked up the phone quickly and trilled a hello. She seemed to be in very high spirits.

"Tippy? It's Myrtle. I was wondering if you had any idea when Palmer Baxter's funeral might be held."

Tippy said in a chipper voice, "Hi Myrtle! When I visited with Shay, she indicated that Cash had been the one who originally was planning the service. When it fell to her, she decided that she just didn't feel up to planning."

"So you're doing it," said Myrtle.

"Yes. Shay seemed rather shaken up by all of the unfortunate events, so I thought the sooner to lay Palmer to rest, the better. I coordinated it with Red, of course. The service will be tomorrow—graveside at Grace Hill cemetery. Ten o'clock."

"Thanks, Tippy. I was certain you'd be the one to ask."

"Talk to you later," said Tippy cheerfully before ringing off.

"Could you hear that?" Myrtle asked Miles.

He nodded. "Like I said, they bury their dead quickly here. Tippy sounded . . . cheery."

"She certainly was. If I didn't know better, Tippy would actually make an excellent suspect. After all, Palmer was encroaching on her territory."

Miles frowned. "In what way?"

"By infiltrating every club and committee in Bradley, North Carolina, and then staging takeovers. Let's face it—Tippy was being displaced. And there's nothing Tippy would hate worse than to be insignificant. Palmer's death must have been a great relief on some level."

"And yet, here she is planning Palmer's funeral."

Myrtle considered this. "I'm sure Tippy is planning something perfect. I suppose we should have asked Shay about the funeral while we were there, but I was focused on other things. I suppose I'd better check and make sure my funeral outfit is in good shape. I swear, the thing is a magnet for stains."

Miles said in a hopeful voice, "So we're just going to wait for Palmer's funeral to speak with Whitley?"

"Oh, I think so. I mean, we could always pretend to be slightly demented—only in the best possible way—and show up at Whitley's with another stuffed toy and pretend we didn't remember we'd just given her one."

Miles made a face. "I don't think I want to engage in that sort of subterfuge. It might be tempting fate."

"Anyway, it will be the perfect time to speak with Whitley. Hiram will be there, too."

"Half the town will probably be there," said Miles gloomily.

"Only if there's free food, which knowing Tippy, there will be. She'll have all the church ladies galvanized. They'll be cooking up a storm in their kitchens and tomorrow there'll be the perfect Southern funeral spread."

Miles frowned. "At Tippy's house?"

"I'm sure it will be in the church hall. After all, Palmer was on a trillion committees there. I'm sure the sexton is already setting up the hall with tables and chairs."

Miles said, "So . . . are we done today, then?" He sounded like someone who got an unexpected reprieve from an onerous task.

"Oh, I think so, don't you? I should probably do other things today. Perhaps I'll start working on my next helpful hints column for Sloan. After all, I promised him I'd submit it as long as I had a byline for a big story. I'll send it along with my write-up of Cash's untimely death."

"I'm sure Sloan will be delighted," said Miles. "What time should I pick you up tomorrow for the service?"

"Let's plan for 9:30. I'll be ready with bells on."

After a peaceful afternoon and evening, Myrtle slept surprisingly well and woke early to work on puzzles and drink coffee. Her funeral outfit had been in perfect shape for once—she'd held it up to the light and scrutinized every inch of it for stains and spills.

However, when 9:00 rolled around and it was time to get dressed, she was shocked to find that the slacks appeared to have shrunk. She couldn't fasten them whatsoever.

"For heaven's sake," she muttered. Pasha, who'd decided to pay Myrtle an impromptu visit, narrowed her eyes at the errant pants.

Myrtle picked up the phone and called Miles. "Let's make it 9:45 for a pickup time. I'm having a wardrobe malfunction."

"Stains on the funeral outfit?" he asked in the tone of someone who had lived through the various sagas of Myrtle's funeral garments.

"No, this time they appear to have shrunk."

Miles paused. Then he said very diplomatically, "Clothes do that sometimes. Is there something else you can wear?"

Myrtle looked through the meager offerings in her closet. "Everything looks very loud. I feel as if I've run into this issue before."

"Perhaps a shopping trip might be in order," said Miles. "The funerals seem to be regular. Actually, they seem persistent."

"I'm not sure my budget will stretch that far this month." She brightened. "But I did have luck a couple of times at the consignment shop. Maybe I should try them out."

"Yes. But not right now because the funeral is in less than an hour."

"Okay. Drive on over at 9:45 and I'll be ready. I may not look particularly funereal, but I'll be in something."

Myrtle tried on another pair of slacks—these were khaki and not particularly appropriate, but they were serviceable. She was shocked to find that those pants had also shrunk. Myrtle frowned. The clues pointed to a slight weight increase. Perhaps all her time at the diner was having repercussions.

She turned a critical eye to the rest of her closet, realizing she'd need to wear a dress. Myrtle grimaced at the possibilities. Then she remembered the golden rule: octogenarians can get away with nearly everything. She pulled out the drabbest dress she could find. It was a faded navy with some sad-looking flowers on it. At least it seemed to fit.

When Miles drove up, Myrtle was outside waiting on him. She climbed into the car and he said, "I have to admit that I'm surprised you're ready."

Myrtle heaved a sigh. "My options were limited. This will have to do."

"I don't think I've ever seen that dress before."

"There's good reason for that. It's at least ten years old and decidedly not my favorite. But, you know—desperate times call for desperate measures."

Tippy, naturally, had made sure that the graveside service was extremely well-organized. She'd put helpful directional signs in the cemetery, directing mourners to the site. When they parked, Myrtle could see the minister, the funeral director, and a woman who was presumably a soloist were already there and waiting.

There were also a fair number of attendees. "Look," said Myrtle. "Nancy is here."

"Nancy who was lent money by Palmer and couldn't repay it?"

"That very Nancy. She may be here for the reception afterwards. I don't blame her. Tippy will ensure there's plenty of food. I might have to wrap some extras in a napkin, myself."

They headed to the back of the tented area and two middle-aged people surrendered their seats so that Myrtle and Miles could sit.

"Age has its privileges," murmured Myrtle smugly.

As with everything Tippy was in charge of, the funeral started on time. The minister greeted everyone and then delivered a eulogy. Noisy sobbing started up and Myrtle turned to see Whitley, standing outside the tent. Hiram tried to direct the very-pregnant Whitley to a seat but she batted his hand away and continued wailing.

When the soloist started singing "Abide With Me," (clearly a Tippy-influenced hymn), Whitley completely fell to pieces and staggered away toward her car. Hiram attempted to follow her, but she gave him a death glare which stopped him in his tracks.

Everyone was looking at everyone else as if trying to decide if someone should perhaps accompany the hysterical, expectant Whitley. Which was when Myrtle rose and quietly slipped from her seat at the back of the tent.

# Chapter Eighteen

Whitley was sitting in the passenger seat of a very large SUV. Fortunately, she'd come well-equipped with tissues and was sitting with an entire box in her lap. She jumped a little when she realized someone was standing there and then relaxed when she saw it was Myrtle.

"Miss Myrtle," she croaked.

Myrtle patted Whitley's hand. "I'm so very sorry. Do you think I could sit with you for a few moments? I think everyone in attendance at the service was most concerned about you. I wanted to make sure you were all right."

"Of course . . . you can sit in the driver's seat," said Whitley. She took another tissue out and scrubbed at her face as Myrtle walked around the large car, leaning heavily on her cane on the uneven ground.

When Myrtle climbed in, Whitley said, "I feel bad about leaving but I just couldn't be there any longer. It was making me so emotional."

"Well, you don't have to be standing right by the grave to show your respect and pay your condolences."

Whitley relaxed a little more at this pronouncement. "Everything has shaken me up lately. It feels like someone is bound and determined to eliminate everyone who was close to Palmer."

Myrtle found this rather an imaginative stretch.

"I wonder if Shay will be next?" fretted Whitley. "What kind of crazy person could be behind this? Plus, the police believe *I* have something to do with Palmer's death. Or Cash's. I simply can't understand why they're asking me these questions." She turned to Myrtle and grabbed her arm. "Tell me if Red has said anything to you about it."

Myrtle gently scoffed, "I never have known what goes through Red's mind, Whitley. Perhaps it has something to do with the falling-out between you and Palmer?"

Whitley drew back in surprise. "People know about that?"

"The gossips in Bradley have been out in full force."

Whitley wavered at this. She didn't appear to want to discuss any sort of disagreement between her and her late friend.

Myrtle said in her most persuasive voice, "One way to shut down Red would be to have a solid alibi for Cash's death."

Whitley said sadly, "I was sleeping soundly for once. I bought a new body pillow and it's helping me sleep harder. I always sleep the hardest right before I get up for the day." In a stronger voice she said, "Whatever people are saying in town about me is a lie. Palmer and I were like peanut butter and jelly—always together. Like sisters."

Then, to Myrtle's extreme discomfort, she broke down into tears again.

At this point, Myrtle was fairly done with crying. She decided she would offer a distraction in the form of asking questions—some of them perhaps pointed.

"I heard that Palmer might have been preoccupied lately. Standoffish."

Whitley, as intended, stopped crying at this. "Palmer?"

It was a complete fabrication on Myrtle's behalf and she wasn't surprised that Whitley questioned it. "That's right. Did Palmer have something on her mind?"

Whitley's pretty face lined with a frown at the question. Myrtle said, "If I can find out who might have hurt Palmer and Cash, the police will leave you alone."

Whitley brightened at this and considered the original question with some fervor. Then she slowly said, "I'd say that she had lots on her mind. Palmer was really in a snit about Tippy."

This made Myrtle raise her eyebrows. "Tippy Chambers?"

Whitley nodded earnestly. "Palmer said that Tippy was used to being the queen bee of Bradley. That she didn't want her encroaching on all of her charity work. Volunteering, I mean." Her eyes grew big. "Could she have wanted to stop Palmer from being in charge of everything? Do you think Tippy did something?"

Myrtle did *not* think Tippy did something. She tried and failed to think of Tippy as a depraved killer. She said, "I'm not sure Tippy would have strayed from the path quite that far."

Whitley nodded, accepting this, and thought again. "Well, if it isn't Tippy and it isn't some crazed person wanting to kill everyone associated with Palmer, maybe it's actually Shay. Because she's going to get all that lovely property and money and whatnot. Maybe she did it for the money."

"Palmer didn't have any other family besides Shay, did she?"

Whitley shook her head. "Not anyone she was close to. There are some random other cousins and an aunt she never liked. Shay was pretty much it. Palmer was very nonchalant talking about it." She looked wistful for a second. "Although part of me hoped that maybe she'd leave me a little tiny something. We were good friends."

Myrtle glanced back over at the graveside gathering. "Perhaps I should walk back over there and stand at the back. I have the feeling it's wrapping up. Tippy would never plan anything that was drawn-out."

"Should I go back over there?" Whitley looked reluctant.

"I wouldn't. Just join everyone in the church hall for the reception—only if you feel up to it."

"Hiram is probably going to want to take me home and have me put my feet up."

Myrtle nodded. "It's not a bad idea. Take care of yourself and that sweet baby of yours."

Then Myrtle headed off to stand at the back of the service until it ended several minutes later. She felt eyes on her and looked around until she saw Red standing across from her, giving her an irritated look. She gave him a blitheful smile in return.

Miles joined back up with her as they headed back to his car to go to the church. "Everything all right?" he asked.

"Fine and dandy. I got Whitley calmed down. She said she was sleeping soundly when Cash was murdered. She also intimated that Tippy might be the murderer."

This made Miles's eyebrows do all sorts of calisthenics.

"I know," said Myrtle. "After Tippy was removed from the list of suspects, Whitley went on to Shay."

"Shay seems to be everyone's favorite suspect."

Myrtle said, "Indeed she is. She does have quite a bit of motive—millions of them, from what I understand."

The parking lot outside the church hall was packed. Myrtle suspected that some of the people showing up for the reception had not been in attendance at the funeral service. Miles, after driving up and down the rows, muttering to himself, finally found a spot to put the car.

By the time they walked into the church hall, there was quite a line at the food table. Myrtle sighed.

Miles pointed helpfully to another food station, greatly ignored, across the room. "Perhaps we should go to that one."

Myrtle smiled. "Ah. Tippy is always excellent at crowd control."

They walked over to the table where the church ladies wielded large serving spoons and generally looked cross. One was looking with narrowed eyes to see if more food was needed.

Myrtle, still thinking about taking some food home, had her plate heaped high with macaroni and cheese casserole, fried chicken, biscuits, green bean almondine, and more. Miles took a more conservative approach and had a couple of ham biscuits.

"I'm not sure your food choices are going to travel well," said Miles as they sat at one of the round tables that was currently unoccupied.

Myrtle smiled. "I decided to eschew the napkin idea." She pulled a small plastic container from her voluminous purse and showed it to Miles.

"I'm not sure that's appropriate funeral etiquette."

"Don't be prudish, Miles. It's not becoming. Besides, there's plenty of food here. Palmer was so involved with the church that the church ladies and Tippy will make sure there's enough for hundreds of people. And there aren't that many people who even live in Bradley."

They ate and looked around them. There were some older people looking rather grim who'd been in the family row at the service. "Those must be Cash's parents," said Myrtle. "I know Palmer didn't really have any family." Her eyes narrowed. "And there's Nancy Young. Let's see if she'll sit with us."

Nancy, however, seemed to be heading for the exit. Her gaze lit on Myrtle's table and then skittered away. She was trapped, however, when Myrtle enthusiastically gestured her over.

"She doesn't seem very excited to be sitting with us," said Miles dryly.

"I saw her put some ham biscuits in her purse. She might have been planning on just slipping out the door with her food and eating them at home."

Nancy gave them a tight smile as she sat down. "Good morning."

"Hi Nancy. Thanks for sitting with us. It's good to see you today. Is it your day off from the store?"

Nancy shook her head. "I have an afternoon shift, so I'll be heading over there in a little while."

"Gracious, but you look tired. Are you doing all right?"

Nancy rubbed one of her eyes. "I just haven't been able to get any real sleep. Red has been coming by to see me. I think he believes I did it."

Myrtle said, "I'm sure he doesn't, Nancy. But you know how the police operate—they have to go through all the motions. Why do you think he's focusing on you?"

Nancy sighed. "He knows I borrowed money from Palmer. And he knows I couldn't pay it back. I've had some hard times—I lost my job right when I had some medical work scheduled. I never could seem to get back on my feet."

"So he's been asking you about Palmer's death?"

"Not just Palmer's—Red's spoken with me about Cash's, too." Nancy rubbed the side of her face.

Miles said, "Do you have a good alibi for Cash's death?"

Nancy gave him a wry smile. "I wish. I was at home when Cash died, but there was no one there to prove it. Just my cats, and cats aren't known for being chatty."

"Did you know Cash at all? Have any interaction with him that made the police think you might be a suspect?"

"None at all," said Nancy, stoutly. "I've never even met the man before. He was never around when I spoke with Palmer. I have to wonder what kind of relationship those two had, considering the fact he was never around."

"What did you make of Palmer?" asked Myrtle.

Nancy gave a little shiver. "She seemed cold to me. And that's not just because she was pushing me to pay her back. Her eyes just had no warmth in them at all. I can't imagine her in a normal relationship with anyone. And yet she was married and had friends, so what do I know?"

Miles said, "Was there anyone you thought could be responsible for either of these deaths?"

Nancy said, "Well, I know Whitley, her best friend, was full of venom against Palmer. I saw Whitley arguing with Cash one day, too. I have a feeling she could have gotten on the bad side of both of them." She glanced across the room and grunted.

"Looks like Shay is coming around and speaking to everybody. I better go."

And with that, she took the remainder of her food and scampered away out of the church hall.

"That was abrupt," said Miles.

"You know, I just can't really see Nancy as a killer, can you? She seems decidedly non-confrontational to me." Myrtle pursed her lips in thought.

"Non-confrontational? But didn't Whitley say that Nancy was driving Palmer crazy by contacting her all the time? Asking for extensions on her loan?"

Myrtle said, "But that's not necessarily out of a drive to confront, is it? That sounds more like *desperation*. Those sound like the actions of a person who doesn't know what else to do. We just saw Nancy flee from Shay, of all people."

"Couldn't that same desperation have driven Nancy to kill? After all, no one is forcing her to repay her loan now. Couldn't killing Palmer have just been a means to an end?"

Myrtle said, "It certainly could have been. But that means she also murdered Cash. It seems a bit extreme for Nancy. I somehow can't see her lurking outside Mariah's house, waiting for Cash to exit."

"It does stretch the imagination a little. So what are we doing next? We'll need to speak to Shay, of course."

"We'll speak to Shay and then perhaps we should leave, regroup, and figure out where to go from here."

Miles cleared his throat. "I hate to mention this, but Red seems to be glowering at you."

"At me? I'm merely attending the funeral of a woman who was active in all of my clubs." Myrtle looked across the room at her son and gave him a steely look in return.

"I think he's just worried about you, Myrtle. It's been a running theme, hasn't it? The medic alert necklace. The warnings not to get involved in the case or to write it up in the paper. I think he just really cares for you."

Myrtle huffed. "He has a funny way of showing it."

They threw away their plates and cups and then spoke briefly to Shay who seemed very subdued and gave them both a hug, which startled Miles a bit. Then they headed for the church hall exit.

On the way, Myrtle spotted Hiram, also getting ready to leave. She said, "I'll meet you at the car, Miles. I'm going to speak with Hiram for a moment. Maybe he knows why Whitley was arguing with Cash."

Miles walked out and Myrtle sidled up to Hiram. "I do think it was a lovely service."

Hiram smiled at her. "I thought the same thing. Palmer would have been pleased."

"Well, Tippy pulled it together and she always does an amazing job with everything she does." Myrtle paused. "I did have one thing to ask you about. As we mentioned before, people have a terrible tendency to gossip in this town."

Hiram lost a bit of color in his tanned face. In a hushed voice after a furtive look around he said, "They're not talking about Palmer and me are they, Miss Myrtle?"

"No, I haven't heard more about that. Perhaps the speculation just petered out. But I did hear something odd about Whitley."

Hiram now looked even more alarmed. "What are they saying about Whitley? Whitley hasn't done anything at all."

"I know, dear, and that's why I wanted to give you the chance to let me counter-gossip by telling me the truth. I hear Whitley had an argument with Cash in his final days. Do you know if that's true?"

Hiram said brusquely, "Of course it isn't true. That's complete nonsense." He paused and then said, "Miss Myrtle, you know I love you. But *you're* not the one spreading these lies around, are you? I always felt you had quite an active imagination."

"Me? Oh, that's silly. I'm simply looking out for a former student, a favorite one at that. If it's not true, it's not true. I'll shut it down when I hear it."

"Thanks," said Hiram, looking a bit more relaxed. After a moment, he said, "You know, Cash was a friend of mine, but he wasn't the greatest guy. I know I've messed up too, but I've never been heartless like Cash. Anybody who would kick out a family member just isn't the most stellar person."

"No, I suppose not. Well, I should join up with Miles—he'll be wondering where I am."

Hiram said, "By the way, thanks for calming Whitley down at the service. That was nice of you. I was going to follow her to the car, but I think she's had enough of me lately. All those hormones have really been acting up."

"Oh, it was my pleasure, Hiram. It was only natural for her to be upset, losing her friend. Take care—I'll see you soon, I'm sure."

But although she moved quickly to the exit, Myrtle wasn't destined to meet up with Miles quite yet. Tippy accosted her. "Myrtle, I'm glad I spotted you."

# Chapter Nineteen

Myrtle said, "Such a lovely service. Palmer would have loved it."

Tippy said absently, "Thank you. I knew Shay wasn't up to having a service and Palmer was so very involved in the town that something needed to be done."

"Are you arranging Cash's, too?"

"No, his family just wants to hold a private memorial service. He'd apparently wanted to be cremated and they said he wasn't a fan of much fuss, so they're keeping it quiet." Tippy, an aficionado of much larger funereal events, seemed rather baffled by this mindset.

"I see."

Tippy continued, "Anyway, I wanted to ask if you could be on a special committee for me."

Myrtle drew back. She knew Tippy's tricks. She was calling it a "special" committee to make it sound more appealing to Myrtle. But it would be a very ordinary committee with very boring meetings, squabbles, and tasks. "Oh, I don't think my schedule would allow it."

Tippy tilted her head to one side as if trying to visualize exactly what Myrtle's heavy schedule might entail. "I'm sorry to hear that you're so swamped right now."

"Yes." Myrtle knew better than to elaborate on her busyness. It would only lead to points where Tippy could argue that the committee wouldn't take much time at all. When dealing with Tippy, it was always best to just tell her no.

Fortunately, Tippy had moved on to another line of thought. "I saw you sitting with Nancy."

"Hmm? Oh, yes. The poor thing. She always has such a tough time, doesn't she?"

Tippy said, "I suppose so. But you know, she can be surprising, too."

Myrtle perked up. The ubiquitous Tippy was involved in everything and was everywhere. She could have valuable information. "Did Nancy act out of character?"

Tippy frowned. "Well, I wouldn't say I know her well enough to be able to comment on her personality. But I found it rather odd that she was arguing with Cash a couple of months before he passed away."

Ordinarily, Myrtle might take issue with Tippy's choice of words. Cash certainly did not "pass away." His life was violently and prematurely ripped away from him. However, she was more interested in Tippy's comment about the argument.

"Was she?" asked Myrtle.

Tippy nodded and frowned. "I've meant to tell Red that. Heavens, I can't believe how the last few days have flown." She glanced around the church hall. "I know I just saw him a minute ago. I should let him know while it's on my mind."

"Oh, I wouldn't worry about that now," said Myrtle, practically purring. "I can pass that along to him. A funeral reception perhaps isn't the best place."

"No, I suppose you're right," said Tippy rather absently.

"Did you hear what the argument was about?"

Tippy said, "I certainly did. Not that I'm the type to eavesdrop."

She wasn't. It was a trait Myrtle had found quite distressing in the past.

Myrtle said, "But there was something different about this argument that you couldn't perhaps help overhearing?"

"That's precisely it, Myrtle. Nancy seemed so distraught and Cash was so dismissive."

Myrtle said, "It sounds like a scene from my soap opera."

"Well, it was quite impassioned. Nancy was asking for money and Cash was just trying to get away from her."

Myrtle frowned. "That's very odd. I understand that Nancy borrowed money from Palmer."

"That's what Cash asked her to do—get in touch with Palmer about borrowing money. He said he didn't do that sort of thing. But his manner was so brusque. It was as if he wasn't even looking at her as a person." Her eyes opened wide. In a hushed voice she said, "You don't think Nancy retaliated against him for treating her that way, do you?"

Myrtle said, "If she did, it was quite a delayed reaction, don't you think? You said Nancy was pleading for money a couple of months ago."

Tippy considered this. "Maybe she just stayed bitter about it. Sometimes things can fester."

Someone called Tippy's name and she said, "Better run, Myrtle. Good talking to you."

Myrtle now realized she'd left Miles waiting for her in the car for quite some time. She hurried out, her cane thumping as she went, to find Miles sound asleep behind the wheel.

She climbed in, waking Miles up with a jolt. Myrtle said crisply, "I certainly hope this nap of yours doesn't continue as you drive down the street. I haven't lived this long by engaging in risky behavior, you know."

Miles rubbed his eyes. "No, I'm wide awake."

Myrtle wasn't convinced. "You have every indication of being very sleep deprived. It's not a long drive. Scoot over and I'll drive."

Miles balked at this, shaking his head. He said, "You don't even have your license on you."

"I *always* have my license on me. And I'm an excellent driver."

Miles, sensing they were going to sit in the church parking lot for a very long time if Myrtle didn't get her way, acquiesced. Myrtle set off at a sedate putter.

"The reason I took so long was because I spoke with both Hiram *and* Tippy. And they were very interesting conversations."

Miles said nervously, "Perhaps we should continue this conversation at your house, Myrtle. I wouldn't want to distract you while you're driving."

"For heaven's sake, Miles! I've been driving since before you were born."

"I don't think *that's* quite the case."

"Near enough. Anyway, Hiram was saying that Whitley absolutely did not have an argument with Cash."

Miles, apparently deciding that no real harm would come to his car with Myrtle driving at a speed he could surpass while briskly walking, offered no further resistance. "Perhaps he's just saying that because he's trying to protect Whitley. Although I can't imagine why Whitley would have been arguing with Cash to begin with."

Myrtle pondered this. "Maybe she found out Cash was having an affair. I can see Whitley being very indignant on Palmer's behalf."

Miles frowned. "And we're to believe that Whitley knew nothing about her own husband's affair with Palmer? It seems to me as if Palmer would be the last person Whitley should have cared about."

"Hiram seemed to believe Whitley didn't know. He said he'd ended things with Palmer because he wanted his marriage to work, especially with a baby on the way. But you're right—what if Whitley realized Palmer and Hiram were having an affair? She might have killed Palmer as revenge and then killed Cash because he knew something."

Miles seemed unwilling to accept that an expectant mother would be quite so brutal. "I like the original idea better—that Whitley was angry at Cash because she heard about his affair."

"I'm sure you do like that explanation. Whether it's the truth or not remains to be seen. Anyway, I spoke with Tippy, too, and she contradicted something Nancy had said."

"What was that?"

Myrtle said, "Tippy said she'd witnessed Nancy having some sort of an impassioned argument with Cash months before he died."

"So Nancy had certainly met him, contrary to what she'd said," said Miles slowly.

"Exactly. What's more, Tippy was able to overhear a bit of their conversation."

Miles raised his eyebrows. "*Tippy* was eavesdropping? It seems most un-Tippy-like."

"She primly stated that she couldn't help but overhear it. She said that Nancy was asking Cash for money and Cash was redirecting her to Palmer."

Miles frowned again. "Okay. So Nancy actually went to Cash first for the money."

"I suppose, like many people, she assumed the husband was the one to ask. That he was the one with the money. It just didn't happen to be the case in this particular relationship."

Miles said, "Well, it all sounds like a very interesting time at the funeral reception. You found out lots of things at the tail-end of it."

"I can't help but feeling as if I heard something very important. But I just can't put my finger on what it is. It's going to drive me crazy. I'll likely wake up in the middle of the night trying to decide what it was."

Miles said, "You'll likely wake up in the middle of the night, regardless." Myrtle pulled up into her driveway and Miles added, "By the way, you might have spilled something on your dress."

"Aah!" Myrtle scowled at her dress. "Funerals are the only times I do this."

"I know. We've eaten at the diner scores of times and you've left unscathed."

Myrtle sighed. "I think this is a sign. I'll go inside and get caught up on my laundry."

"Good idea. The way things are going, you'll be needing funeral attire again soon."

Myrtle went inside and started with the laundry, using a fair amount of stain remover in the process. While the load was in the washing machine, she worked on another story for Sloan, this time a profile on Cash. Fortunately, Cash seemed to have a robust online presence and Myrtle was able to get lots of details about his work without making any phone calls.

She heard a scratching sound and turned to see Pasha staring at her through a window.

"Pasha! You're trying to get my attention, aren't you?" Myrtle let her into the house and Pasha came in, looking pleased.

"Food?" asked Myrtle. "Has it been a slow hunting day?"

Pasha was quite the talented huntress, eliminating a large part of the rodent population of Bradley. She had been focused on birds for a while but, perhaps sensing Myrtle's displeasure, turned to rodents and reptiles. There wasn't much she could do when there was nothing to hunt, however.

Myrtle said, "You look a bit crestfallen, Pasha. Don't worry—it's not you. I suspect that the rodents now have some sort of early-warning system if you're in the area. That's why tuna was invented."

Myrtle realized she would save a significant amount of money if she bought cat food. She usually did have cat food in the house, but she'd forgotten it the last few times she'd been at the store. Tuna was pricey and frequently *Myrtle's* lunch. However, since she was just supplementing Pasha's diet, she didn't go through too many cans.

Pasha attacked the paper plate of tuna with gusto as Myrtle settled back down again in front of her computer. When Pasha finished her meal, she wandered back over to give herself a bath near Myrtle.

Myrtle frowned. "Pasha, I still have that feeling I missed something important today at the funeral. Someone told me something that doesn't quite fit in."

Pasha closed her eyes halfway as if trying to help Myrtle figure it out.

"I spoke to a few people. Nancy, Hiram, and Tippy. I don't care what people say, I just don't think Tippy is a killer. Of course, if she were, she'd be the most organized killer in the history of crime."

Pasha appeared to agree with this.

"So what did Nancy and Hiram say? Nancy is apparently lying to us. She said she didn't know Cash, but she knew him well enough to ask him for money. Then Hiram and I talked and he seemed more concerned about people gossiping about his affair with Palmer than anything else. Still, there was something there in those conversations."

Pasha pondered this, eyes now completely closed.

Myrtle decided to go back to writing her article, hoping the forgotten clue would come to her as she worked. Pasha decided to sleep on it.

Later, Myrtle moved on from the article to evening game shows. And from game shows to her book. When it was quite late and she was rapidly filling in a crossword puzzle, her doorbell rang.

Pasha growled and immediately slid under Myrtle's sofa.

Myrtle frowned. Miles was more likely to come over at three than he was at one. At one o'clock in the morning, it was hard to tell if you had insomnia or not. At three o'clock, it was all very clear. She moved toward the door. But looking out, she couldn't see anyone.

Myrtle continued scowling. Was some teen out playing tricks on her? "Most vexing," she muttered.

And not at all conducive to heading off for a sound sleep. Pasha came cautiously out from under the sofa and huddled near Myrtle. "Do you want to have a sleepover?" asked Myrtle in surprise. The cat, feral as she was, rarely wanted lengthy interaction.

Pasha looked meaningfully into Myrtle's eyes, signifying her consent.

Myrtle was turning off lights and was in the kitchen to make the coffee for the next morning when she heard a scrabbling sound at her back door. She narrowed her eyes. "We're going to put an end to this foolishness." She opened a drawer and pulled out a lead-crystal candlestick that had been part of an ill-fated set she'd received as a long-ago wedding gift.

Pasha bounded into a dark corner, putting her back against it. Her green eyes glowed in the semi-darkness.

The back door, after more jimmying sounds, flew open.

Myrtle raised her candlestick but it was knocked out of her hand by some sort of stick. Which was when she saw Hiram there, holding a golf club.

# Chapter Twenty

"Hiram!" said Myrtle in her best schoolteacher voice. "What in heaven's name are you doing here?"

Hiram sighed. He looked just as regretful as he did back in the day when he would admit he hadn't completed his homework assignment. "Miss Myrtle, sometimes we have to do things we don't want to do."

"Yes, Hiram, I realize that. There are plenty of things people do that they don't want to do. Exercise. Their taxes. Visiting the dentist. But most people wouldn't put killing octogenarians in that category."

Hiram gave a humorless laugh. "I'd forgotten how sharp you are, Miss Myrtle. Or maybe I made the mistake of thinking you had gotten duller with age."

Myrtle said with a sniff, "I do the crossword puzzle every day, Hiram. And I knock out the cryptic crosswords in mere minutes."

Hiram nodded. "That's what I'm saying. If I'd thought about that at all, I wouldn't have spent so much time talking with you. When you came to the golf shop, I would have just deflected any questions. Instead, I sort of thought it was cute that you were so nosy. I didn't realize how dangerous you were."

"Until the funeral reception? That's when you knew."

Hiram sighed. "That's when I understood that you knew. I wasn't totally sure *how* you knew and I wasn't sure if *you* knew that you knew."

Myrtle paused for a second to work through all the "knews." Then she said, "It was when you said that bit about Cash kicking out Shay, wasn't it? That clicked in my brain, although I was wracking it earlier today to try and remember what had struck an off-note. Shay wanted that to be a secret because it embarrassed her. She's had some experience being homeless and she didn't want to return to that state. Cash and Shay were the only ones who knew about that."

"Except, obviously, you," said Hiram, a hint of admiration in his voice.

"Precisely. I'd been over at Shay's house to see her after Cash died and saw all the boxes. She had to tell me. But the only reason you'd have found out is if Cash told you. And you swore that you hadn't spoken to him after Palmer's death because you weren't sure what to say. You'd contradicted yourself."

Hiram swung the golf club absently. "There was a little saying you had. You'd bring it up in class when someone would try to explain why they didn't have their homework. It was about lying."

"It's 'If you tell the truth, you don't have to remember anything.' Mark Twain."

Hiram gave a rueful nod. "I should have memorized that one."

Myrtle put her hands on her hips. "I see that you're planning on murdering me, Hiram, but it seems to me that you're going about it a very silly way." She gestured to the club. "You're going to beat me with that? I'd think forensics would be able to figure out it was a golf club. You'd be the primary suspect as the local golf pro."

Hiram frowned at this. "I guess I didn't consider that."

Myrtle said, "If you'd just smothered me in my sleep, no one would have thought anything about it. Old lady dies while sleeping. End of story."

"That's very true. I wish you hadn't asked so many questions, Miss Myrtle. I've always respected you so much."

Myrtle said crisply, "More than you did Palmer and Cash, I suppose."

"I'm not sure what I was thinking to get involved with Palmer. Maybe I was just flattered."

Myrtle said, "Here's what I think happened, Hiram, and you can tell me if I've gotten it wrong. I think you *were* flattered by Palmer's attention. You had an affair with her. But then your conscience intervened and you realized you wanted to start anew with Whitley. You have a baby on the way. You told Palmer it was over and she balked at that."

"She wasn't used to being dumped."

"I'm sure she wasn't," said Myrtle. "Perhaps she threatened to tell Whitley about the affair, out of spite. It seems like the sort of thing Palmer would do."

"I told her it would mess up her relationship with Cash if she told Whitley. That Whitley would be sure to fill Cash in about the affair. But she didn't care. Palmer had the money and the control, she said. And she knew Cash had been cheating on her, too. She had plenty of leverage."

Myrtle said, "You were horrified at the thought of Whitley finding out. Maybe Palmer had told you previously about her plans to approach Bo at the diner and try to pressure him into selling the business to her. You knew Whitley wouldn't register that you were even gone that early because she was exhausted."

Hiram nodded, silently, looking as if it were a relief to hear it all outlined when it had been a jumble in his head.

Myrtle continued. "You followed Palmer out to the diner before it was even dawn. You approached Palmer's truck while she was reaching in gathering her papers. Then you spoke to her. She probably thought you were trying to persuade her again not to tell Whitley—to keep your secret. Palmer turned away from you and you struck her from behind with something you grabbed from her truck."

"A bag of canned goods," said Hiram quietly. "You know, I think of it as self-defense, Miss Myrtle. Obviously, not physical self-defense, but to preserve my life with Whitley."

"A very self-serving explanation," said Myrtle in a crisp voice. "Then there was Cash, your alleged friend. He clearly found out about the affair between Palmer and you—perhaps while he was clearing out Palmer's things. Maybe there was a note on her calendar? Some sort of evidence of the affair, at any rate. Cash realized you had quite the reason to kill Palmer. Maybe he called you up and accused you of having an affair with her."

"I told him we didn't have an affair at all. That it was just a flirtation and that it was over. But Cash wasn't so sure. He said something like *I'll have to ask Whitley about that.*"

Myrtle nodded. "I rather thought so. And that sealed his fate. You already knew about Cash's affair with Mariah. You waited for him to leave her house and then attacked him at his car. The same M.O. you had with Palmer."

Hiram gave a short laugh. "But you don't have a car, Miss Myrtle. So I had to think outside the box." He took a small step toward her.

Myrtle took a step back.

Hiram said, "We already know how this is going to go. How about if you make it less-traumatic for me by making it easier?" He moved toward her, now a bit more menacingly.

Which is when Pasha started caterwauling. Myrtle had forgotten the black cat was there and jumped a bit. Hiram whirled around at the odd, penetrating racket. Which was when Myrtle pressed the button on her lovely medic alert necklace.

She wasn't sure how long it would take dispatch to answer and was surprised when it was immediate. "What's your emergency?"

Hiram whirled around again, his face pale. "Where is that coming from?" he gasped.

Myrtle peered at him. "Are you hearing things, Hiram? Perhaps it's the ghosts of murders past."

Hiram took a few steps backwards. Pasha continued to make absolutely blood-curdling shrieking sounds.

"Make it stop," said Hiram, glaring at Pasha.

Myrtle said complacently, "If you understood feral cats, you'd know you can't make them do anything."

There was a sudden ruckus at Myrtle's front door.

Hiram growled, "What's going on here?" He shoved Myrtle forward through the kitchen and to her living room, which is when her front door burst open and Red, wearing sweat pants and a tee shirt, exploded inside. To his credit, Red took in the entire scene—the golf club, the threatening ambiance, and Hiram's increasingly despondent countenance and pulled a gun out of his pocket.

"Gracious," said Myrtle. "Do you *sleep* with guns, Red?"

"Just thought one might come in handy when dealing with you, Mama," said Red, his voice just the tiniest bit gruff. "I just never know what I might be facing."

Hiram, realizing the gig was finally up, sank down on Myrtle's sofa as if his legs weren't able to support him any longer.

# Chapter Twenty-One

The medic alert monitoring service had not only immediately called Red (it notified the closest relative on record), but had also put in calls to police, fire, and EMS. Which is how a host of emergency vehicles, including Red's on-call deputy, had descended on Myrtle's small home in the middle of the night. Hiram was placed in handcuffs and taken away.

Most annoyingly, Erma had come over, gaping, to ensure Myrtle was all right. This time, even Red was ready to see her go. "She's just fine," he'd told Erma, effectively shutting the door in her donkey-like face.

Miles was over directly after Erma, blinking in the lights of the assorted emergency vehicles. Red pointed him over to the kitchen where Myrtle was having a large cup of coffee. "Coffee?" she asked Miles in a chirpy tone.

He nodded, looking relieved. "I thought something horrible had happened to you. But you seem just fine."

"*I'm* just fine. Hiram is another story. He'll be carted off to prison for quite a long time."

She was about to launch into the story when Lieutenant Perkins arrived, looking crisply professional in white button-down and pressed dark slacks.

"Lieutenant Perkins," said Myrtle with delight. "Good morning to you! Can I get you a coffee? I'm just about to pour Miles one."

"How about if I fix us both one, Mr. Bradford?" said the policeman. He did so, quite competently.

"Where did Red go?" Perkins asked, glancing around him.

"Oh, I think he probably felt a bit underdressed, considering how nice you look. I'm guessing he headed home to put on his uniform."

Perkins nodded. "It's a good thing he came over like he did. That was quick-thinking on your part, Mrs. Clover."

"Wasn't it? Wanda told me to keep that necklace close, and I listened to her. It saved my life."

"Wait, wait," said Red, hurrying over. He'd apparently put on his uniform in great haste because the buttons didn't line up the way they were supposed to. He sat down at the table with his mother and said, "Okay, shoot. I want to hear how you busted this case wide open."

Myrtle, looking hard for it, found a glint of admiration in his eyes, buried under a few other feelings. She said in a self-satisfied voice, "Well, earlier today, I'd commented to Miles how I'd felt I'd learned something important at the funeral reception."

Red muttered, "Somehow you always seem to get clues at funerals. I should start tailing you."

"Perhaps you should," said Myrtle with a sniff. "Anyway, the problem was, Hiram realized I knew something."

"When you were speaking with Hiram at the service," said Perkins.

"Precisely. Although I suppose it didn't completely register with *me* until later. I knew I'd heard something important but couldn't put my finger on what it was."

Miles said, "But Hiram realized you knew something."

"He did. He broke in through the back and was planning on killing me with a golf club. I told him it was a really terrible plan."

Perkins said, "Hiram would have been the top suspect if forensics had said you were murdered with a golf club. Did you remember what you'd found significant at the funeral?"

Myrtle nodded. "After I saw Hiram at the door. I realized he'd talked about Cash and how heartless he was to throw Shay out of the cottage. But Hiram had said earlier that he hadn't spoken with Cash after Palmer's death."

Red muttered, "He'd contradicted himself."

"Exactly."

Miles said slowly, "So Hiram murdered Palmer—but why?"

"Well, if you remember, Hiram was trying to start his marriage anew with Whitley. He envisioned a happy family of three and Palmer didn't figure into the picture. But Palmer, as Hiram explained, wasn't exactly used to not getting her way. We knew that when we heard how determined she was to buy the diner from Bo."

"And turn it into a French café," said Red, rolling his eyes. "So Palmer was unhappy with Hiram for ending it. Was Hiram saying she attacked him, and it was self-defense?"

Perkins said thoughtfully, "Or was Palmer planning on exposing the affair as revenge?"

Myrtle beamed at Perkins as if he were a star student. "You guessed it. Palmer wanted to make sure Whitley knew about the affair. She knew that would stymie Hiram's plans to rebuild his marriage prior to the birth of his first child."

Red said, "Wait a minute. What kind of idiotic plan was that? Whitley would have surely have informed Cash that Palmer and Hiram were having an affair. It would have harmed Palmer and Cash's marriage."

Myrtle shrugged. "Hiram said that didn't matter to Palmer. She knew Cash was having his own affair with Mariah from the diner. Plus, Palmer was the one with most of the money in the relationship. It apparently gave her a sense of security."

Perkins took a sip of his coffee. "So Hiram sneaked out early to follow Palmer to the diner, clearly knowing about her early meeting. He killed her to keep her from divulging the affair. But what about Cash? Did he find out something that didn't add up?"

"It was more that Cash discovered Hiram had a good motive for murdering Palmer—the fact they were in a relationship. He wasn't aware of their affair until he was going through Palmer's things and came across evidence of it. Then Hiram staked out Mariah's house, waiting for him to exit."

"And his next stop was *your* house," said Red darkly.

"He was very determined to keep his family intact," said Myrtle.

"Well, it's a good thing you were able to call for help, Mrs. Clover. You not only escaped from Hiram, you've ensured he'll be behind bars for a long, long time," said Perkins.

He stood and Red followed suit. Perkins said, "Guess we should be heading out to question Hiram now and hear what he has to say. Thanks for your help with the case, Mrs. Clover, as always."

Red winced a little at hearing his mother's name in the same breath as *case*. But then, perhaps, also relieved that the investigation was over, he said, "I do have a present for you, Mama."

"Another one? And here I was thinking my necklace was so special."

Red nodded. "A different sort of present. I was talking to your neighbor, Erma, yesterday afternoon."

"Poor you."

Red continued, "She told me she's got to get bunion surgery done today."

"Why are you regaling me with this horrid information, Red?"

He smiled at his mother, his eyes crinkling. "Because she's having the surgery done in Charlotte and will stay there with her family for several weeks to recover."

Myrtle and Miles stared at each other; eyes wide. Then a large grin spread over both of their faces.

Perkins chuckled. "It sounds, from what I've heard of Erma, like a wonderful holiday."

And it was. After the police left and they'd both cobbled together some sleep, Myrtle and Miles found themselves on Myrtle's front porch again, eating tomato sandwiches, drinking lemonade, and counting cars.

# About the Author

Elizabeth writes the Southern Quilting mysteries and Memphis Barbeque mysteries for Penguin Random House and the Myrtle Clover series for Midnight Ink and independently. She blogs at ElizabethSpannCraig.com/blog, named by Writer's Digest as one of the 101 Best Websites for Writers. Elizabeth makes her home in Matthews, North Carolina, with her husband. She's the mother of two.

Sign up for Elizabeth's free newsletter to stay updated on releases:

https://bit.ly/2xZUXqO

# This and That

I love hearing from my readers. You can find me on Facebook as Elizabeth Spann Craig Author, on Twitter as elizabethscraig, on my website at elizabethspanncraig.com, and by email at elizabethspanncraig@gmail.com.

Thanks so much for reading my book…I appreciate it. If you enjoyed the story, would you please leave a short review on the site where you purchased it? Just a few words would be great. Not only do I feel encouraged reading them, but they also help other readers discover my books. Thank you!

Did you know my books are available in print and ebook formats? Most of the Myrtle Clover series is available in audio and some of the Southern Quilting mysteries are. Find the audiobooks here: https://elizabethspanncraig.com/audio/

Please follow me on BookBub for my reading recommendations and release notifications.

I'd also like to thank some folks who helped me put this book together. Thanks to my cover designer, Karri Klawiter, for her awesome covers. Thanks to my editor, Judy Beatty for her help. Thanks to beta readers Amanda Arrieta, Rebecca Wahr, Cassie Kelley, and Dan Harris for all of their helpful suggestions and careful reading. Thanks to my ARC readers for helping to spread the word. Thanks, as always, to my family and readers.

# Other Works by Elizabeth

**Myrtle Clover Series in Order (be sure to look for the Myrtle series in audio, ebook, and print):**
Pretty is as Pretty Dies
Progressive Dinner Deadly
A Dyeing Shame
A Body in the Backyard
Death at a Drop-In
A Body at Book Club
Death Pays a Visit
A Body at Bunco
Murder on Opening Night
Cruising for Murder
Cooking is Murder
A Body in the Trunk
Cleaning is Murder
Edit to Death
Hushed Up
A Body in the Attic
Murder on the Ballot
Death of a Suitor
A Dash of Murder
Death at a Diner
A Myrtle Clover Christmas (late 2022)
**Southern Quilting Mysteries in Order:**
Quilt or Innocence
Knot What it Seams

Quilt Trip
Shear Trouble
Tying the Knot
Patch of Trouble
Fall to Pieces
Rest in Pieces
On Pins and Needles
Fit to be Tied
Embroidering the Truth
Knot a Clue
Quilt-Ridden
Needled to Death
A Notion to Murder
Crosspatch (late 2022)

**The Village Library Mysteries in Order (Debuting 2019):**
Checked Out
Overdue
Borrowed Time
Hush-Hush
Where There's a Will
Frictional Characters
Spine Tingling

**Memphis Barbeque Mysteries in Order (Written as Riley Adams):**
Delicious and Suspicious
Finger Lickin' Dead
Hickory Smoked Homicide
Rubbed Out

**And a standalone "cozy zombie" novel:** Race to Refuge, written as Liz Craig